BLUFF & CO.

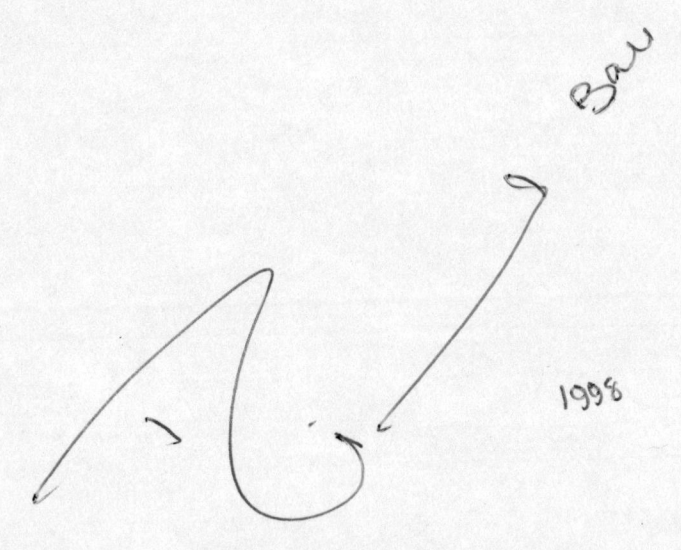

With best wishes

[signature] Bav

1998

By the same author

Traddles & Co.

BLUFF & CO.

Richard Ball

Illustrations
Paul Barham

Merryvine Publishing Ltd

" Bluff & Co." is a work of fiction: names, characters, places and incidents either are the product of the author's imagination or are used entirely fictitiously. Any resemblance to actual persons, living or dead, is purely coincidental.

Published 1996 by Merryvine Publishing Limited PO Box 240, Godstone, Surrey, RH9 8YH, England

Copyright © Richard Ball.

The right of Richard Ball to be identified as the author of this work has been asserted in accordance with sections 77 and 78 of the Copyright Designs and Patents Act 1988.

A copy of this book has been lodged with the British Library.

All rights reserved. No part of this publication may be reproduced, stored in a retrieval system, or transmitted in any form or by any means, electronic, mechanical, photocopying, recording, or otherwise, without the prior permission of the publishers.

ISBN 1 900087 01 4

Typeset by Power Plus Publicity Ltd, Oxted, Surrey
Printed and bound by Biddles Ltd
Guildford, Surrey

To Andrew and Erica
For their love and caring of all God's creatures

Acknowledgements

To Pam Hillyard for unscrabbling my manuscripts and making them readable.

Sue Miles " the old biddy" for making the adventures in this book come true.

Mike Van Boolen for his invaluable help and advice in all we do.

To the following for their equine assistance:-

Jane Edwards
Sue Mather
Jane Soulsby

and to Peter Cook for his help with the bantam.

Thank you.

Chapter 1

A Fond Farewell

The day had come at last! Retirement! The four pit ponies were old friends and had worked nearly all their lives down the Judy Shirley Coal Mine in the North East of England. They were both excited and anxious for this was their last working day down the pit. They had known for a little while they were to have a long rest, after the man they knew as the "horse doctor" (the vet), had decided that for them, mining was over.

The leader of the group was Bluff, known as a Cream Dun, due to his creamy beige coat, black eyes and dark brown mane and tail. He stood some twelve hands or 120cms (48") high. He had been working in the mine for twenty-five years.

Bobby and Bruce were brothers, Welsh ponies both grey, with black eyes and light manes and tails. Taller than Bluff, they stood about thirteen hands or 130cms (52") high. They too had worked for twenty five years in the Judy Shirley and were inseparable. They even shared the same stall for which special approval had been given.

The fourth member of the group was Don, a small Shetland pony who was entirely black with bright black eyes. He was a mere ten hands 100cms (40") tall and had been working in the mine for some eighteen years. Although younger than the other three, Don had "got the dust", the dreaded disease suffered by some miners from working down the pit. They inhaled coal dust which coated their lungs and were then left with breathing and chest problems. Don had been diagnosed with the same condition and it was agreed that he too should be retired.

The pit ponies had arrived at the mine, which was located in Northumberland and extended under the North Sea, when they were four years old. After several weeks training on the surface, their days were spent with their own miner driver, usually on a seven and half hour shift, pulling and pushing tubs of coal along the roads down in the mine. Sometimes they took along material for roadway repairs and on other occasions they removed the rubbish from the airways. They had even worked in places where machinery could not reach.

They were housed in warm, dry stables down the mine, lit with electricity and located for safety reasons out of the way of the busy underground main roads. After the big strike in 1974, however, all the Judy Shirley pit ponies were always housed on the surface. There, they could be looked after whilst the strike was in progress as no one was working down the mine. The Judy Shirley was a shallow pit. There was very little variation of temperature above and below ground (as is usual with deeper coal mines), so the ponies' health did not suffer by their going to their quarters "up top."

On this, the start of their last working day, the hooter went as usual; the signal that meant the miners were to go to the cage in the lift to travel underground. The ponies having lived on the surface for a spell recognised the call to work and waited to be taken down the mine.

Whilst they worked pulling the coal tubs along, all the ponies wore a special harness. Made of leather, its main purpose was to give maximum pulling power to the animal with the minimum of discomfort. It was also worn for the pony's protection and safety. It fitted over the animal's head with protective side shields over the eyes and a cap passed between the pony's ears and joined the broad harness band around its neck.

Unlike usual horse-drawn equipment, the shafts of the coal tub were attached to the harness by chains joined by a thick leather band to form a 'U' shaft. The band was then attached by a hook and eye and secured with a pin to the coal tub. After the day's shift, the detaching device was removed from the hook and eye and the pony and limber (the attached shafts) came free from the coal tub. Often a pony would be required to change tubs during a shift and with that type of harness, it could be done very quickly and easily.

All the ponies were fond of their miners who treated the animals with great kindness and affection. Bluff felt sad about leaving Ivor who had been his friend for nearly the whole time Bluff had worked underground.

Ivor and Bluff hitched up to the coal tubs and commenced their work. Bluff made quite sure, however, that there were only eight buckets to be pulled. If anyone dared to put on nine, he refused to move! Ivor knew how Bluff felt about the matter so he made quite sure that there were only the usual number.

Ivor told Bluff how much he would miss his working partner after that day's work and went on to say that he too would be retiring shortly. He added that as both he and his pony had worked hard down the mine they both deserved a rest. Bluff listened intently just in case Ivor knew where Bluff and his three friends were going. All four pit ponies were thrilled that they were to be retired together but they did not know where they were going, or with whom - so Bluff tried to hear as much as he could, hoping to know where their new home would be.

Meanwhile, Don, who was known as the "Billy Bunter" of

the quartet, was busy heaving trucks with Charlie, his miner driver. Don had a reputation for eating anything that was offered to him and Charlie used to get very upset with his miner colleagues when they poked fun at Don for eating so much. Charlie had to admit, though, Don was getting a bit fat. The small Shetland pony, however, was not bothered about what was said of him; he was only interested in what the miners carried in their tuck boxes and if their wives had remembered to pack a little extra morsel or titbit for him! Charlie his miner spent most of his time in the Miners' Club and often came to work with a very sore head and a firm declaration that he would "not touch another drink!" Don knew Charlie never meant it but on their last day together, Charlie was very sad that he was going to lose "Old Greedy" at the end of the shift. He appreciated what the "horse doctor" had said though. If Don were left underground any longer, he would not survive. He realised Don had to be retired for his health. Charlie knew he would miss his friend very much.

Bobby and Bruce, the greys were rather "stand-offish" ponies and as brothers they were as different as chalk to cheese. Bruce was the outgoing one who took everything in his stride but Bobby was highly nervous and until he knew people well, he treated all of them with great suspicion.

Bruce's driver was Ernie who loved the ponies because as he said, he played the ponies every day when he placed a bet on them at the bookies! Bruce always knew when Ernie had picked a winner and equally when Ernie had lost all his brass! Ernie was a real gambler and he would bet on anything, win or lose. He always thought the next time would be his lucky break but of course it never was.

Syd, who worked with Bobby, was a very quiet fellow who

was proud of his garden but he kept himself to himself. He did not readily make friends with the other miners; it was perhaps for that reason that Bobby, his pony, was a loner. Although Bruce, his brother, felt he could carry on working for another twenty five years, Bobby was tired and eagerly looked forward to the whistle which signalled the end the shift.

All the ponies and their miner drivers worked steadily through the day and at last the final whistle could be heard. Once free of their harness, the ponies clocked themselves off and then, two at a time, stood head to tail, corner to corner in the cage that carried them to the surface where they knew a man waited for them. As was their daily routine, the ponies were taken to their stalls, brushed down and rugged to save them catching a cold after sweating underground. Their miners then hurried to the changing rooms for their baths. In the meantime, the ponies were given a good feed of oats and nuts and they soon relaxed.

About an hour later, Bluff heard that a man from the Pit Ponies Protection was coming to see them. The ponies knew that group of people well because they often visited them in the stables and in the pit to see that they were being well cared for. The ponies always received something tasty whenever a visitor came along from that organisation. It would appear that the latest arrival was a very important person and would be accompanied by a senior official from the Coal Board who would explain where all four ponies would be sent. Bluff readily passed all that information along to his friends and a deep discussion between them followed as to where they might be going. All were agreed that it was very good they were to be together and one by one, the ponies gradually fell asleep - dreaming of green fields and sunshine.

Chapter 2

En Route

Early the next morning, a large horse lorry drew up outside the stables and the four ponies, each wearing headropes or halters, were loaded on board.

Bluff was quite excited about where they were going; Don was content just to look around to see if there was anything he could nibble. Bobby and Bruce were having an argument because as usual, Bobby was in a panic, a complete bag of nerves, and Bruce was telling him to behave and not to be so silly. Bruce was not at all bothered about their journey and although his working life was behind him and he had enjoyed it, he was now looking forward to his freedom.

The lorry did not travel far - merely to the Coal Board's stables just outside Newcastle. The four friends recognised the buildings because they had spent all their summer holidays there in the green fields, under the trees. They always looked forward to their visit to the country when the mine closed down for the annual break in August.

When pit ponies were retired, they were held in the stable areas attached to their particular mine. On the horse doctor's instructions, they were slowly put out to grass to get them used to the change from the pit, in readiness for their permanent retirement on the surface. As the little group were led down from the lorry, they saw how green the paddocks looked and drank in the fresh air. Don could not contain himself. All that rich grass was too much for him and he found himself being told off by Bluff for being too frisky!

The ponies were taken to newly painted stalls and were all given a hay net. Don was heard to mutter "... this is the life" as he tucked into the sweet hay which was hanging up for him.

Later in the morning, the stable staff started to clean and tidy the stalls and the ponies realised that something was about to happen. Bluff looked out of his stable and saw a long line of "special" people approaching. He called to the others and in consequence, every stable door had a pony's head over the top - well nearly every stable door because Don was still inside munching! The other ponies persuaded him to leave his beloved food and he tried to poke his head over the door and peer out at the small procession coming down the path.

The visitor from the Pit Ponies' Protection was no less than one of its Trustees and very distinguished he looked too. The ponies realised that the man knew all about them and that he was really a friend. The representative from the Coal Board was very cordial and when the little party reached the stalls where the pit ponies were, they stopped and discussed each animal in turn. The 'Captain', (the man from the Protection) showed great interest in each of them and raised a number of queries about their present health, how long they had worked, their temperament and their suitability to go to one of his retirement centres in the country.

Bluff, of course, was very dignified. Don nuzzled the Captain to see if he had any titbits to eat and the two greys acted true to form with Bruce, everyone's friend, and Bobby trying to hide in a corner of the stall. The onlookers noticed that Bobby was rather shy and Bruce wished he could make all those people understand that he would look after his brother wherever they went. Bluff was straining to hear the conversation and where they were going; he hoped the Captain would not split them up after all. Bluff felt sure the Captain understood the ponies and would ensure they could stay together.

The horse doctors decided that the four would start off with one hour a day in the paddocks which would gradually be increased until it was safe for them to eat grass. Bluff was most excited because he had heard that he and his friends were going to a farm in Surrey owned by the RSPCA. Just where Surrey was, or how far, he had no idea but he was cheered all the same. He knew it was no use telling Don because immediately the small black pony would want to know how much grazing there would be - and Bluff did not know; so he told the greys and instantly Bobby was panic-stricken. It took another telling-off from Bruce to settle him down. Bruce was quite cross and told his brother what a big baby he was!

Don, as usual, was the one who moaned about the time they had to graze in the paddocks and when evening came, he was given a hay net to finish off the day and declared that he was almost starved!

All the ponies had a medical and Bluff was quite pleased with his result from the horse doctor who declared that he had never seen such a healthy pony. Bruce and Bobby were declared fit but the doctor considered they were a little underweight. Don's diagnosis was that he was too fat and a strict diet was drawn up for him. The doctor already knew that Don had "got the dust". He also confirmed that the black pony had a touch of laminitis, a blood condition, usually found in older ponies, caused by the animal eating food too high in protein, like rich grass. The animal's blood became over-rich and if the pony then became hot, he was often unable to walk and required special treatment. In Don's case, the doctor said he might have to have horseshoes to strengthen his hooves. When he heard the doctor explaining his condition, Don felt that all medics should be abolished and no one, but no one, would cut his food down. His continual groaning about that "rotten doctor" irritated his three friends. He also wondered what horseshoes were. He caused so much fuss that Bluff felt duty bound to find out for him.

The next exciting thing to happen was when the Captain came to ask if he could be provided with photographs of the four ponies in their working harness, pulling tubs. Bluff looked forward to dressing up and rather fancied himself in his harness. Don hated the leather skull cap they wore, although he forgot the many times that it had saved him from serious injury in the past years. Bruce took it all in his stride and wondered why anyone should want to take pictures of him. Bobby went into a real sweat and thought it was a trick to get them to work down the mine again. He swore never to trust the Captain from that moment on!

The day of the photographic session dawned and the four ponies were duly harnessed up and led into the yard where the coal tubs were waiting. A man with a camera was dashing around and the ponies had to pull the tubs on to some waste ground because the photographer wanted the background sets to be authentic. Perhaps the people there understood him but none of the ponies did and even Bluff began to think it was a waste of time. The ponies did not mind having photographs taken at all, as long as it was quick but the stupid man just did not know when to stop. As he tried to pull Bluff around to get the best light, the old pit pony trod on his foot! As soon as the photographer cried "whoa", all the other ponies looked over to where Bluff stood and then realised

Bluff was trying to control his mirth. It was not long before the foolish man started to hop around on his uninjured foot, using the sort of language the miners used when they had their feet trodden on!

Apart from the light relief of the photographic interlude, life for the four ponies settled into a very relaxing routine. They spent their days either eating or sleeping, with Don continually moaning about the small amount of grazing they were getting. That did not bother his three companions and the time passed gently by until Bluff started to worry, thinking that the promise of going to the country had been forgotten. He began to get agitated and the thought of stopping in the stable block forever started to depress him. He became short tempered with his three friends, especially with Don. The two greys felt that the Coal Board centre was as far as they were going. Bobby had quite made up his mind that they were not moving on. Bruce noticed that his brother was not so nervous about their situation. Bluff's abrupt attitude and impatience, however, was something they all had to contend with.

Then one bright morning, all the heads (apart from Don's) peered over the stable doors to see a large group of strangers walking towards the stable block. The ponies were getting used to seeing people of all shapes and sizes, with their different clothes of varying colours. They had only been used to looking at the miners in their orange working attire and had never seen a "lady person" until they had left the Judy Shirley Mine to start their retirement. As a lady approached, they all felt at a loss and Bobby fled to the rear of the stall and broke out into a sweat. Bruce was upset by Bobby's persistent questions, asking what was happening; Bruce was having difficulty working things out for himself. Don could only hear the noise of the approaching group and queried it with Bluff, who snorted that Don would have to wait and find out in due course like the rest of them! That remark was so unlike Bluff, who really did not know why the people were coming but his mane started to twitch with excitement. He had been on edge recently but suddenly, it seemed that something could be happening after all. The booming voice of the Captain could be heard above the general buzz of conversation and Bluff understood that the large number of people, especially the "lady" ones, were from the Captain's Pit Pony Committee. They had come to see the ponies before they left for the country. In the group were Coal Board officials and union members who were there to organise the farewell arrangements. Bruce said he heard something called "television" mentioned and Bluff retorted that if that were anything like the man who had recently taken their photographs, a few more toes might be trodden on - accidentally of course!

The ponies soon retreated to the backs of their stalls to escape the constant rubbing of heads, and twitching of lips that so many of the people present were doing to them. Bobby was so scared that he never went near the door anyway but Don endured it all and found some of the fingers grabbing at him contained food. Eventually, even he had to give up and withdraw to the back of his stall. Bluff and Bruce giggled about the number of fingers they had inadvertently nipped, or the sleeve of a cardigan or coat that had caught in their teeth.

After a lengthy discussion with the Committee, the Captain then said that everything was ready at his animal home for the ponies and all that was required was the vet's agreement stating the ponies were fit to travel. The farewell arrangements were to be organised and the Captain concluded by saying that he would like the four miners who had worked with the ponies to be present when the ponies left the Coal Board stables for their onward journey to Surrey. When they heard that announcement, the four friends were delighted as they had not seen their miner drivers since their retirement day at the Judy Shirley. Bluff would be with Ivor once more and Charlie would join "Billy Bunter" and the two greys would meet Ernie and Syd again. Bobby wondered if Syd would come and say goodbye - Syd was never keen on crowds or pomp, as he called it, but even so, Bobby hoped his former working partner would turn up for a last farewell.

The officials eventually departed and the Captain returned to the stable block with his 'treats for the lads.' All the ponies liked the Captain enormously and afterwards agreed that they could not have a better person to take care of them. Even Bobby surprised his three friends by giving the man a friendly nudge. They heard the Captain say that from then on, the four of them were going to enjoy their days at his farm.

On the first day of October, exactly two months after their last shift underground, the four ponies were taken from their stables to be groomed ready for the farewell ceremony. Although they were combed and brushed frequently in their working lives, the ponies did not appreciate their beauty treatment that morning, but when they realised that they were going to their retirement place, they became impatient to 'get on with it.' Bobby soon relaxed, which surprised Bruce, who knew that his brother could go into one of his nervous spasms and create problems for the stable lads. Bluff was excited and apart from turning around to nip the backside of the lad grooming him, he took all the beauty treatment in his stride. Don felt that all the combing and brushing was quite unnecessary and when his lad wanted him to raise a foot, he stubbornly refused. He put his weight on that particular foot which had to be prised off the ground. The boy gave him a prod in the ribs which soon caused Don to change his mind and he stood still. Brand new halters were then fitted to the ponies and they were led up to the exercise yard where a large crowd of people had assembled. Bluff was quick to pick out Ivor who came running across and threw his arms around his pony. Don was soon reunited with Charlie and Bobby was touched to see that Syd, his miner, had arrived after all and made a big fuss of his "silly old grey" as he called him. Bruce and Ernie were rejoicing at their meeting and Bruce was pleased that his friend had remembered to bring a few sugar lumps. The four ponies stood with their miner drivers, all very pleased to be together again - for a short time anyway. The Mayor was there and he read out a letter from a Mr Joe Gormley, who was the President of the Mineworkers Union, praising the four ponies for their devotion to duty and explaining how the animals had worked for all those years under the North Sea. Mr. Gormley, in his letter, went on to say how very proud of the ponies he was and they were true brothers of the Union. The only thing they did not have was a vote!

All the onlookers enjoyed those remarks but the ponies were getting a little fretful and started to paw. Many cameras could be seen and there were television lorries everywhere. The ponies were having 'hero' treatment which they did not understand. It seemed like an eternity before all four were led into a gleaming, newly painted horse box with the floor thickly covered with straw and a very large helping of hay, which of course pleased Don. Ivor, Charlie, Ernie and Syd came up to say their goodbyes and the ponies noticed the tears and the choked up voices, a trembling mouth and a discreet use of the handkerchief as each miner gave a fond farewell to his pony. Bluff had a lump in his throat and the greys huddled together, feeling very forlorn at that moment. Don gave Charlie a quick nudge and returned to the important task of eating! Bluff really told him off; but Don with a mouthful of sweet hay could not think of anything better to do just then, and carried on chewing.

All the ponies were then walked up the tail-gate at the back of the lorry, tied up and made safe for the journey and amidst loud cheers from the large crowd which had gathered, the lorry moved off. The ponies could hear a lot of hip-hip-hooraying which became faint as they drove on and then there was just the sound of the engine.

Chapter 3

Journey's End

For the first hour or so of the journey, the four friends discussed the ceremony which none of them really understood but it did seem to please the large number of people who had gathered together that morning.

Bluff was thrilled that Ivor had been there and Bobby remarked that having Syd stand by his side made the day much easier for him. Don could not understand why so many people wanted to get up on a platform and talk about what the ponies had been doing. Bruce suggested that that was the way people did things and went on to explain that at union meetings underground, everyone wanted to say something and if it were good, all the other men assembled there would clap their hands together and make a terrible row. Sometimes, when the men shouted at each other, they did not clap but would raise their hands in the air, with more cheers and shouting. Bobby said that it was a good job ponies did not smack their hooves together or put them in the air when they were annoyed! Bruce retorted that if ponies did that, they would all land on their backs and his brother was stupid for saying such a thing! Bobby felt hurt for he rarely offered an opinion and then when he did, he was ridiculed. He decided to sulk and took no further part in the discussion.

Bluff thought the flags were colourful and the miners who had made the music had really tried hard. Don mentioned he had heard that the band was famous and the type of music played was especially for occasions such as the ceremony that day.

Another topic of conversation was that the driver of the horse box was in fact wearing his best suit and the ponies decided that perhaps it was something to do with people having their pictures taken by the television cameras. With the steady hum of the lorry, the discussion died down and the ponies were all lulled into a snooze, each immersed in his own thoughts. Bobby was thinking what a rotten lot the others were, always poking fun at him; he then broke into a cold sweat when he thought of the place where he was being taken. He wished he and his friends could have stayed where they were for at least they knew everybody there; and with those thoughts whizzing around in his mind, he felt more and more depressed. His head hung very low and if he could cry at that moment, he would.

Bruce looked across at Bobby and thought that his brother had gone into one of his depressions. Inwardly Bruce felt sorry for Bobby because as he often said to the others, it must be awful to be so nervous all the time. Bruce himself was bored and the lorry ride seemed to go on forever. He wondered if they would ever stop.

Don felt hunger pangs and decided that travelling in lorries should be compensated by a large helping of hay. He tried to think of other things but all his thoughts returned to hay, corn, grass, apples and carrots and he stamped his feet in utter desperation.

Bluff was a great dreamer and he could stand for hours reminiscing and chuckling to himself about the many amusing things that had happened to Ivor and himself over the years. Time never meant much to Bluff - he learned to shut it out from his mind, thus defeating boredom.

The lorry suddenly stopped and the ponies came back to reality with a start. The driver could be heard at the side of the vehicle. There was a clanging noise as he lifted out buckets that had been set in a small compartment there. It was at that moment the ponies realised how thirsty they were and when he appeared with the buckets full of cold, clear water, all thoughts of monotony disappeared from their minds.

After having a good long drink, the driver gave each animal a nose bag and then muttered something about how hungry he was - which caused Don to exclaim that if the driver thought he was hungry, he should have known how Don felt! The food was very welcome and helped to quell the nervous tension that had been gradually creeping in. Bobby decided to eat his food very slowly and savour every morsel, whilst Don had quickly finished his and was throwing his head up and back to dislodge any grain that had stuck to the bag.

Having made sure the ponies had something to eat, the driver then started his own lunch. He turned on some music which the four ponies could hear quite clearly in the back of the lorry. All agreed it was not unpleasant to listen to. An hour later, the driver came and removed the buckets and unhitched the nose bags.

It gave the ponies quite a jolt, with Bobby going wobbly at the knees when the driver started the lorry's engine again. The vehicle moved off very smoothly and the animals all settled down to the rhythm of the engine and the general sway in the back. Suddenly, they heard the most awful noise and realised it was the driver trying to sing! To make matters worse, it was out of tune and sounded just like a grater. When a miner sang down in the mine like that, it was just a noise. He would often get his toe trodden on or be knocked off his balance by the offended pony pulling the tub. The lorry driver was rendering an old pop tune at the top of his voice which was more than the four passengers in the box at the rear could bear. Bluff immediately took the initiative and told the others to start kicking and dancing in protest. Bobby thought a good whinny would help deafen the noise. Bruce agreed. All hell was then let loose with the ponies stamping and snorting and neighing as loud as they could. The poor driver wondered what had happened and pulled over to the hard shoulder. He jumped out of the cab and rushed around to find out if the ponies were all right and what had caused all the din. Mysteriously, as soon as the singing had stopped, the clamour from the four friends ceased. The driver was very puzzled. He could find nothing. He scratched his head, returned to the cab and pulled away to continue the journey south. As soon as he began singing again, there was an immediate response from the passengers. The competition between the ponies and the driver went on for some twenty miles before the driver eventually was forced to give up. He could not hear himself above all the banging and shrill cries from the rear. He never did discover what had been the cause of the fracas and the journey continued in peace for all concerned! The ponies then settled down, each wondering what the end of the drive would bring for them. Bruce mentioned that it would have been interesting if they could have seen outside the lorry, which prompted Bobby to say he was glad he could not see out as it would have made him more nervous. Don agreed with Bobby because he knew that once he saw green fields rushing by, which meant food, Don would have been miserable. Bluff chastised Don saying he had a one-track mind. Don retorted there was very little else a pony could think about and Bluff had no answer to that remark. The four companions then agreed that at least they were all together. Retirement had not parted them after all.

Bruce asked Bluff if he knew what the RSPCA was for and Bluff replied that as far as he could understand, it was a society which had a good name for caring for animals such as themselves, although he did not know exactly what the initials stood for. Don felt that the animals under the care of the RSPCA would probably be able to eat as much as they wanted and was immediately told to be quiet by the others. Bobby wondered what a "farm" was, having heard Bluff say that they were going to a farm. Bluff really did not know but considered it was something to do with pit ponies. He did not want to tell Bobby that he had very little idea -which prompted Don to accuse Bluff of that very fact! Bluff became quite irate and turned on Don, demanding whether the black Shetland knew. Don said that he did not know what the word meant and with that, all the ponies became quiet for a spell.

The discussion soon started up again with the friends reminiscing on old times at the mine. The lorry droned on. Bluff suggested that they should all try and get some sleep so that when they arrived, they would be fresh and alert. The driver was feeling tired himself and it was getting dark. Trying to find a small village in the South of England in the gathering twilight was no joke. He had never heard of South Bunford which was near Tilchester, a small town situated at the foot of the North Downs. Twice he stopped and asked the way and became very annoyed when the people he questioned obviously could not understand his Geordie accent. At his third attempt he was finally directed to the right road and a short while after, he pulled into a drive with a sign saying "RSPCA South Bunford Animal Sanctuary." He was pleased to see that there were lights on in the building and people waiting.

Inside, the ponies felt the lorry slow down and come to a halt. They could hear voices. The only one they understood was that of the driver. Don wondered what language was being spoken. Bluff said he did not know but it sounded most odd to the four friends. The back of the lorry was lowered and one by one, the ponies were led out into the yard. It was cold and the driver pointed out to the waiting group that the journey had made the ponies "sweat up" and they should be taken to the stables quickly. When they reached their living quarters, the ponies were all surprised at how spacious the stables were. On the wall was a net full of lovely smelling hay and Bluff knew exactly what was happening in the next stall occupied by Don. In fact, the chomping from Don's jaws could be heard quite clearly. When Bluff asked Don how he liked his accommodation, all he could hear was the sound of munching! The two greys were having words about their new home. Bobby said he would never settle down to living there and an exasperated Bruce snapped at him, saying that if Bobby did not keep quiet, he would not stay with his brother. Bobby complained that he did not want to come to the farm in the first place and Bluff could hear the exchange between them as he closed his eyes for the night. Bobby and Bruce eventually nodded off and the only sound that could be heard was Bruce complaining that Bobby had taken up all the room! From Don's stall, was a steady breathing - obviously contentment from a full stomach!

Chapter 4

Hello Stranger

Bluff was suddenly awakened by a strange noise. He whipped his head round and saw a most weird looking creature sitting on the door.

"Who-who are you?" he asked with some trepidation.

"Why?" answered the 'being' on the door.

"Well, I've never seen anything like you before," said Bluff.

"And I have never seen anything quite like you!" was the reply.

"I am a pony of the working variety!" retorted Bluff, trying not to be too sarcastic.

"And I am a bantam of the chicken variety" responded the creature, at which Bluff felt that he had lost a battle. The bantam was also a resident of the Sanctuary and Bluff thought him to be too full of his own importance.

"Let me tell you" went on the bantam "I have lived in your stable for several weeks now and I feel a little upset that you have taken over my abode!"

"You can still live in here with me" volunteered Bluff "in fact, a bit of company is always welcome!"

"Do you snore?" enquired the bantam.

"No, I do NOT!" gritted Bluff and turned away with utter disgust as the horrid little feathery bird strutted up and down on his door. He felt like charging over and knocking him off and would have done so too but inwardly he was a little scared.

The noise and chatter had awakened Don who tried to look over his door but as with his previous quarters, he was too small.

"Who are you talking to?" he asked Bluff.

"Oh, some cocky little upstart called a bantam" returned Bluff.

"Knock him off your door!" suggested Don.

"I don't think that will solve anything" retorted Bluff who still did not look at the intruder. The bantam meanwhile considered that the new occupants of the stable were not very friendly first thing in the morning and he decided to fly down to the flower beds and scratch for whatever he could find.

Bruce and Bobby, both with their heads looking out of the doorway, decided that they would not in any way become involved with that impertinent creature.

After a while, the ponies all dropped off to sleep again. They were tired from the long journey of the previous day. Everything seemed so quiet.

"So you are Bluff are you?" Bluff nearly leapt out of his skin.

"Who in the name of thunder said that?" he wondered and turned his head towards the voice. There stood a fair-haired lady person with a very kind face and a smile beaming from ear to ear.

"I'll ignore her" thought Bluff "and she'll go away!"

"So, you're the famous Cream Dun from the Newcastle Mines are you?" the voice cooed.

"Famous" thought Bluff. News must travel fast and with compliments like that, how could he ignore the girl so he thought "I'll just wander over and grab her hand!" B A N G!!! Bluff saw stars. All he had done was to catch her hand and WHOP, she had caught him fair and square! He leapt back in

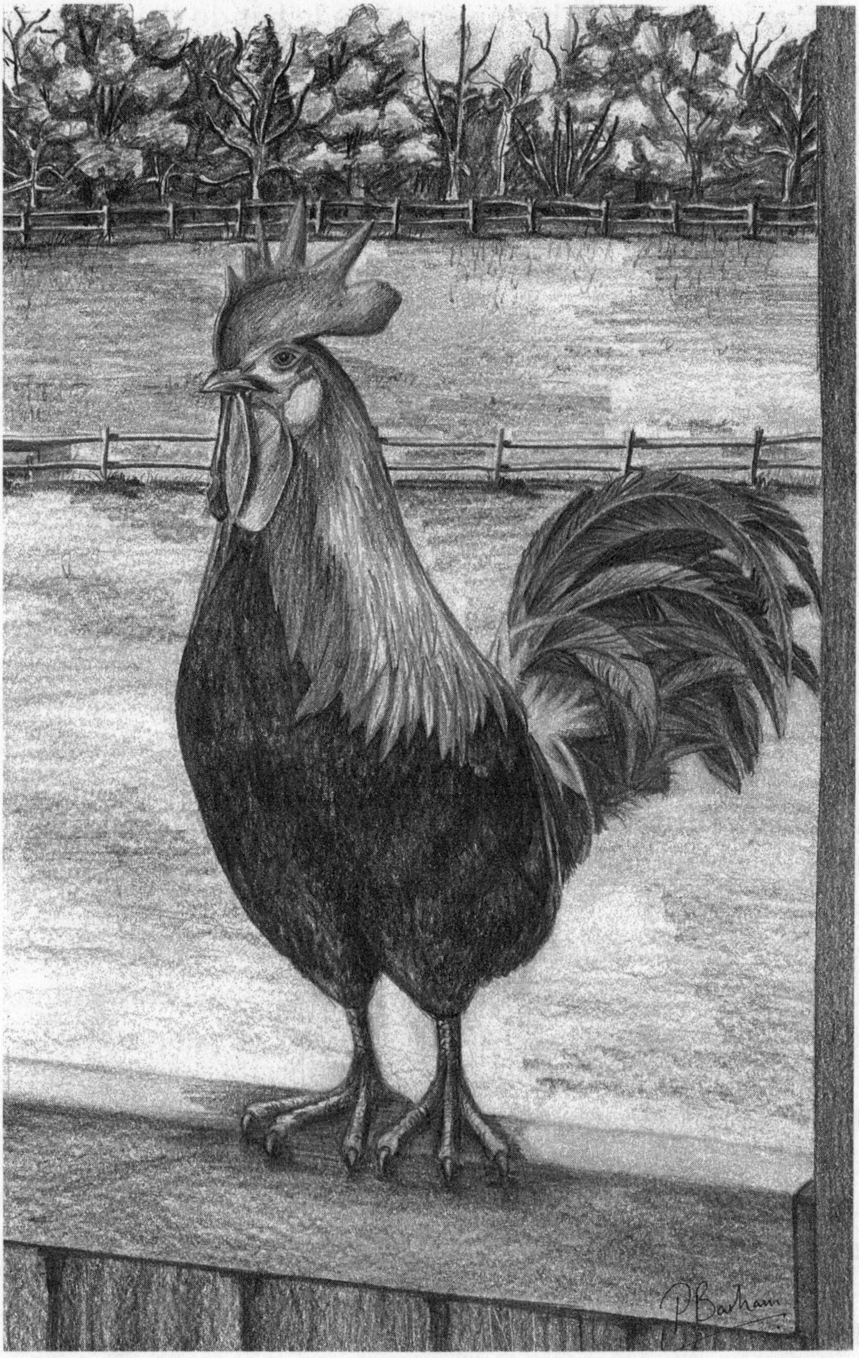
P Barham

utter amazement. What on earth made her do that? It was only a bit of fun thought Bluff.

"Ponies do not bite young ladies!" the voice said "especially young ladies who come to work early to see the ponies she is going to look after!"

"Look after?" thought Bluff "this person is going to look after us? Never! She'll get her come-uppance! Fancy bopping me, a poor old pony. Besides, she talks funny AND smells funny. She doesn't smell at all like the miners used to." (Secretly, he liked the smell but no way was he going to admit it to her.)

The other ponies, seeing Bluff's dilemma, did not even try to go over to the girl. Even Don thought twice. After the young lady left the ponies settled down to discuss the morning's events. Firstly, they had met the bantam who had done nothing to impress them. Then, they had the encounter with the girl who said she was going to look after them AND who could not even take a friendly gesture without retaliation. As Bluff reminded the others, it had all happened to him! The greys had decided that they would sooner have stayed where they were and Don did not relish the fact that if things were going to be strict, then his chances for an extra bit of food would be slim. A great hubbub outside drew the ponies to their doors and the sight that met them nearly sent Bobby into a frenzy! There were several of the type of people like the lady who Bluff had met that morning, all dressed the same in blue tunics, dashing around with different animals. The lawns outside the stables were covered with them. Very soon Don's door was opened and the fair-haired girl entered, holding a new sweet smelling hay net. "Morning Don" said the voice. "You're a handsome looking fellow! I hope you don't bite like him next door!"

"Bite?" thought Don "not when you're bringing in food - and besides, you are quite right I am very handsome! I can't see why Bluff didn't get on with you - and you don't smell too bad really! Well, it's a smell that grows on you I expect!"

The greys stood back when the girl went into their stall. She felt Bobby's flanks and said "I see you need a special diet. You are both too skinny!"

"Tell her I need a special diet!" shouted Don to the greys. But they never replied. They were both very scared, although she was soft and gentle with them.

"Don't trust her" called Bluff. "She'll come at you when you are least expecting it!" Bobby found refuge in the nearest corner whilst Bruce pretended that he was tough and in no way afraid of a mere slip of a girl like this.

A little later, a rather portly person looked in at the stables and the girl who was to look after them asked if the vet would see them that day. The man spoke with authority, as if he was in charge of the Sanctuary and acted rather 'importantly.' "Twit" thought Bluff and like the other three, completely ignored him, even when he leaned over the door and pleaded for them to take notice. The man even pretended to Don that he had food in his hand and was rejected by the black pony.

"You'll have to get some weight off him" he said to the girl. That remark not only brought tears to Don's eyes but also made him more resolute to dislike "Old Portly" from that moment on.

After breakfast the four ponies were led by their halters to a hitching post, on the edge of an enormous lawn. It was their first glimpse of the environment in which they would now live. To be truthful, they were all impressed because for years they had only seen or been used to a small area and all the stable yards had been tiny compared with what met their eyes now. Everything was clean and neat and beautifully laid out.

It was a great treat to see and the ponies were impressed by its tidiness. Don said he could smell the sweetness of the pastures already and Bluff tutted and turned his head away. His main thoughts were on the girl who had unceremoniously boxed his ears earlier. Evil thoughts raced through his mind as to how he could get his revenge. That opportunity came about five seconds later when she came up and decided to clean out his hooves. She bent over and lifted the front nearfore foot and started to clean the muck out. Bluff turned his head very slowly and with one quick and considered movement, sunk his teeth into her bottom!

"Oh, my God!" she yelled, as she leapt about two feet in the air, with both hands holding the injured area. "You rotten thing. Just you wait!!"

Bluff, through his own tears of joy, could see that she had tears of anger as she hobbled away to get treatment for the injury. All the ponies rolled up with mirth at the limping girl as she disappeared from view. "Well," thought Bluff "one all!" and he felt more relieved at having his ego restored. "She won't try me out anymore" he mused "and I think I'll be able to hold my head up again." Don looked over at his old friend with that 'hero' look and the greys thought he was really brave to have a go at "Madam" - who earlier had tried to frighten the lives out of them and in the case of Bobby, succeeded.

Little did they know that already Susan, for that was the girl's name, was preparing her own campaign. Returning from being 'patched up,' Susan walked up to Bluff, who was indulging in a little smug complacency and took him by the halter and looked him straight in the eyes and said "My name is Susan. I have been told that I am to look after you and look after you I will. If you think for one tiny moment that you are going to lead me a life of misery by constantly fighting, then my lad, you had better think again!"

Bluff knew by the tone that the girl was really angry and his complacency left him like a shot. His legs felt a little lumpy and from the vicious look in the girl's eyes, he knew she was not joking. He looked across at his friends and not one of them gave him any moral support. Their pride of a few moments ago had changed into an attitude of "don't bother us, you caused the problem so you get on with it." What could he do but lower his head and hope she would drop into a big hole. Susan limped about and ordered him to "lift your foot" and lift it he did. When he looked around a second time, immediately she shouted "You try that again and I will pole-axe you!"

"Whew" he thought "she is really cross" and Bluff stared to the front as though she had just shot him.

Don looked across with a knowing look in his eyes "I bet he will do everything she tells him in future" he thought whilst the greys pretended that they were nothing to do with Bluff. Without any more ado, Susan cleaned all the feet and painted them; she combed all the manes and tails and gave the four ponies a jolly good groom and not one word or deed of revolt was uttered by any of them.

One by one, the ponies were led in front of a very distinguished looking man who they knew from their previous experience was the horse doctor but known at the Sanctuary as 'the vet.' One thing that amused them was the fact that he did not wear glasses like ordinary humans but a single glass. Every time he raised his eyebrows, the glass fell out and he spent most of his time putting the glass up to his eye! Bluff was first. The vet, called "Mr Harry", listened to his heart and lungs; he watched as Susan walked Bluff up and down; he looked at the pony's teeth, in his ears and under his tail. Bluff was very pleased when Mr Harry said that for his age, Bluff was in splendid health and could go out to grass for an hour or so. This could then be extended each day until he became used to it. Old Portly, who stood with the vet, beamed with delight and nodded to Susan to bring Don over. "Oh dear" thought Don "here we go again -put him on a diet -that's all he will say.." and true to form, Mr. Harry prodded Don's tummy and said to Old Portly: "You've got to get some of this off" and to Susan he added "put him in the field for no more than an hour and let him have a small hay net."

Don was astounded. "How I hate vets" he thought. He stamped his feet with disgust as Susan led him up and down in front of Mr Harry. Mr Harry shook his head and turning to Old Portly said "He has laminitis of the front hooves. I suggest the farrier places light-weight shoes on the front. That will help him but the real answer is that we must get some of this weight off." Don was flabbergasted. All anyone could say was "Get his weight off..." Did they never think of him as a pony. The day anyone said "feed him" would come as such a surprise he would most probably pass out. The whole human world was hell bent on starving him out of existence, Don was convinced of it.

Bobby was next and he had worked himself into such a sweat that the vet told Susan to rug him. Apart from being so nervous, Mr Harry thought Bobby was in pretty fair form. "He does want building up though" advised Mr Harry. "I suggest sugar beet pulp as a start." Don's eyes nearly popped out of his head when he heard the vet's pronouncement. "Why couldn't he have said that to me?" he wondered.

Bruce stepped up full of confidence and was called "Old fellow" and all such endearing names which tempted Don to call out "Crawler" but he resisted the temptation. Once again, sugar beet pulp was ordered and Don decided to shut his ears to any more of the conversation. He was utterly convinced that this so-called vet was another "quack doctor" whilst his three friends were very impressed with the way they had been examined. When Don tried to gain sympathy from the others, he was quickly put in his place so he kept quiet. Susan had also been instructed to worm the ponies and the vet said he would give them a "flu jab." Generally, he was impressed with them all and to Susan he said that Don was "an excellent little fellow." Don never heard that (having retreated from the conversation); if he had, it might have put him in a better mood.

As soon as the vet left, Susan told Old Portly, the Manager, that she was going to put the ponies out to graze for a short while because, after all, they had been cramped up for a long time on their journey and "a taste of freedom may do them some good."

Bluff was the first to go out and he set quite a trot. The girl did not know if it was because he wanted to get to the field, or to get away from her! Bluff felt it was a bit of each. As soon as he was free, he bucked and kicked and galloped as fast as he could and the paddocks were so large that it seemed as though he was running forever. He stopped and saw Don and the greys also entering the field and as soon as they were free, all hell let loose as they too experienced liberty and the open air. Don was the first to stop and start munching followed by the others. My goodness the grass tasted good, clean and fresh and all the ponies relaxed as they grazed.

Their time was over far too quickly and it was Bluff who

suggested that they lead Susan a merry dance. As one, they galloped away as she approached. The trouble was she never panicked - she merely followed them. The first to be caught was Don because he could not resist a further mouthful of succulent grass. Next to fall prey to this tedious person was Bruce who felt that he had had enough running for one day. As soon as he was caught, Bobby went to pieces, neighing all over the place. That crafty girl had left the gate open and silly Bobby followed her and Bruce right into the stable. Bluff was furious! What could he do on his own? He stood in the field for ages and she never once came back. "Why was this?" he wondered. Slowly he meandered up to the gate - pretending to graze and still she never appeared. Bluff felt like neighing but thought better of it and stayed around the gate for over an hour before she re-appeared. The old pony was so pleased that he had not been forgotten, he actually walked up to her and in return she put her arms around his neck and for a few seconds they stood as she hugged him. "Gee whizz" thought Bluff "it's a good thing the others never saw this!" Secretly, he was glad that Susan and he would now get on. "After all," he thought "she smells better than the fellows we had!" and together they walked into the stables, Bluff with Susan's arm around his neck. As she took off his halter she gave him a kiss on the head and left the stall.

After a while, Bruce called out to Bluff. "Hey, you want to watch that lady person. She gives kisses as she put us in our stalls!" Bluff did not answer. In a way, he was feeling a little hurt that what he thought was something personal to him, was in fact the property of all the ponies. "Anyhow, Bruce always did have a big mouth" thought Bluff.

The ensuing conversation centred around the size of the paddocks and the amount of grass that covered them. Don reckoned there was enough food out there to last him for life. Bruce dampened his spirits by saying that according to the vet, Mr. Harry, Don would not be seeing much of it! Bobby rather liked the fact that the paddocks were completely surrounded by trees and once in the fields it seemed that one was in another world. All the ponies agreed that from the point of view of comfort, this was paradise which tempted Bluff to remark that they had moved from "Pit to Paradise."

That afternoon, the ponies were visited by the Captain who, as usual, had a pocket full of titbits. Susan was with him and told him how Bluff had bitten her. Poor Bluff thought that he would surely get reprimanded for his misdeeds but instead the Captain almost doubled up with laughter and caused Susan some embarrassment when he suggested she should show him where the offence occurred. "Poor girl" thought Bluff "she has gone a bright shade of red." The Captain could not get over the fact that the old war horse had attacked in such a devious way. Bruce heard the Captain say that they would be having a welcoming ceremony with lots of publicity - whatever that was, and the ponies spent quite a time trying to work out what the word "ceremony" meant. Don volunteered that it sounded like extra food and was quickly rebuked by the others. Bobby thought it could be something to do with the vet and was accused of being "vet mad." Bluff suggested it might be like the thing that happened to them when they left the stables at the mine "with music and all that." As none of them had a better idea, the conversation came to an abrupt halt and they all lapsed into a "pony nap."

A sudden flapping of wings and Bluff was brought back to reality with a jolt for lo and behold, there, sitting on his door was the cocky little bantam who had so rudely spoken to him that morning.

"Watcha ugly" said the bantam "I hear you had a run in with the biddy who looks after you then."

"Clear off" retorted Bluff.

"Oh, I see" taunted the bantam "she got the better of you did she?"

"No she didn't" replied Bluff "and for your information, she is not a 'biddy' as you call her."

"Well, just you wait until you get to know her" the cocky little devil snapped and then started to preen himself. This was too much for Bluff and he whipped across the stall and with a whack of his nose, pushed the bantam off the door. The noise was awful.

"You stupid clot" he squawked "you could have killed me!"

"Well, don't come round my stable with all your airs and graces" snapped Bluff. "The way you act anyone would think you owned the place!"

"Well, I did before you lot arrived" was the reply.

"Well, you don't now" retorted Bluff.

"Does that mean you'll not allow me to roost in here with you then?" enquired the bantam.

"You can roost in here as long as you don't get too cocky" said Bluff and the cheeky little bird fluttered up to the rafters and had a quick look around.

The other ponies wanted to know what all the rumpus was about and Bluff explained about his lodger.

"Kick him out!" called Don.

"Yes, tell him to go" urged Bobby.

"He won't take any notice" said Bluff. "We'll just have to put up with him.

"OK" ventured Don "but kick him when you get the

chance!"

Bruce looked out from his stall and noticed that the clouds were thickening and there was rain about. No wonder the bantam came in early. Bruce never did like rain and it would appear from what he had heard Ernie say a long time ago that "rain and greys do not go together." He turned to Bobby and mentioned the prospect of rain and he saw his brother visibly shiver. They stood very close together and that was how Susan found them when she came to give them their afternoon feed. She had soaked the sugar beet pulp well and the smell was delicious. There was a big hay net which she had hung on the wall and she checked the water bowl. Neither of the ponies trusted her yet and waited for her to leave the stall before they went over to eat. The smell of the pulp wafted into Don's stable and he realised how hungry he was! Susan came in with a small hay net and Don didn't even wait for her to fix it to the wall before he started pulling the hay from it. "Hey, hold on there" cried Susan "I know you are hungry but let me finish tying the net before you start eating it! At this rate you'll try to eat my arm" she added warily. Poor Don was so hungry he could have eaten anything and to think all he was to have until tomorrow was one small hay net.

Bluff snorted as Susan brought his net and wished she could understand him as he could understand her; but there it was - humans did not understand animals and could not converse with them as he could with his friends.

"Goodnight everyone" called Susan as she prepared to go off duty. The only answer she received was from up in the rafters - "Clear off, you silly old biddy!"

Bluff was furious and the other ponies took a dim view as well. "If you are going to stay in our stables" shouted Bluff "then you'll temper your language."

"Sorry" said the bantam "but I always say the same to her and she always smiles, so I thought she liked it."

"She doesn't understand you" Bluff told him "and the noise you make seems to her to be something nice. So from now on if you can't say anything reasonable, don't say anything at all! Understood?"

"Aye, aye, Captain" crowed the bantam and Bluff just snorted thinking "stupid bird."

The evening conversation was mostly about the first day in the Sanctuary. As Bruce pointed out, there was not a lot to be said about one day, especially as so much of it was spent in finding out about the place. They all agreed that the pastures were excellent and the amount of room they had was good. Bluff considered that Susan would turn out to be "really super" but Bruce felt she could well be a little too sentimental. Bobby was absolutely scared stiff of her. Bluff could not understand why because it was with him she had been cross. Don thought he may well be able to acquire extra rations from Susan but he was not sure whether Old Portly might stop it! They all laughed at the vet and the glass he wore in his eye. None of the ponies had seen anything like that before.

As evening drew on, the clouds thickened and the rain that had been threatening earlier started. All the ponies stood at the back of the stalls and each one noticed that although the weather was cold and miserable outside, the stables were snug and comfortable. Bluff stretched out on the nice warm peat that covered the floor and was quite at home. Soon the greys were lying down and nodding off. Don remained standing. He did not think he would dare to lay down in case he did not have the strength to stand up again! From the rafters came the soft clucking as the bantam lived through some of the day's adventures he had experienced with the other bantams and chickens in the Sanctuary. It must have been very late when a light was shown through each stable door and Old Portly looked at the ponies to make sure all was well. Bluff noticed how wet the man looked and was glad that he at least was warm, dry and very comfortable. "Goodnight" called Old Portly. But there was no response and his voice was heard talking to his dogs as he walked away with them towards his quarters. All the ponies were too tired to talk anymore and quiet came to the stable block.

Chapter 5

A Rude Awakening

Bluff was awakened very suddenly by a S-c-r-e-e-c-h and there was the bantam perched on his doorway. Dawn was only just breaking. The poor pony felt that he had only just dropped off.

"Come on you lazy lot" shrilled the bantam "time you were up and at it!"

"I'd like to be at you" grumbled Don as he changed feet "you are the noisiest lodger in the world!"

"Who's got his hind feet in a twist then?" cooed the bantam, continuing his preen.

"Why the dickens do you have to get up so flipping early?" complained Don "surely you could have a little consideration for others!"

"Consideration is what you want do you?" retorted the bantam "if you four old codgers went to sleep earlier then you would be up and about like me!"

"Why don't you just push off!" murmured Bluff sleepily.

"All right, all right, I know when my welcome has been out-worn" and with that the bantam flew from the door out into the rain.

"I wonder what he does all day?" thought Bruce, still annoyed at being awakened so early.

"Why don't we throw him out of the stables?" asked Don, as he foraged around his stall hoping to find a spare morsel of hay he might have overlooked the previous night.

"How can we do that?" queried Bluff.

"Easy" responded Don "just get him in reach and with a little flip of the old hind legs, lift him out of the stall!"

"You can't do that!" Bobby chirped up "he's far too fast for that. Whilst you are sizing him up he would be away!"

"The only thing we can do" volunteered Bluff "is to have a good talk to him tonight and strike a bargain with him."

"Suppose he won't" said Don.

"Then we'll kick him out!" snapped Bluff.

At least the bantam had provided a good topic of conversation between the four and Bluff felt that it was better that they vent their feelings on him and not on each other. After all, it is a trying time when one moves home and tempers could get frayed.

As it was still very early, the greys tried to nod off but Don's continued walking up and down in his stall put a stop to that. Noises around the centre started up and Bluff, looking over his door, saw a very big chicken type creature go up to the bantam and give him a thump. Bluff excitedly called out to the others. "Quick, have a look at old cheeky getting walloped by that bigger fellow!" The greys could see quite easily but Don was having a job because of his small size. "Where, where?" he kept calling out. "Over there" replied Bluff, but it was no good. Don could not see anything. Meanwhile, the bantam was side stepping the bigger bird very well but as the three ponies knew, he was on a hiding to nothing. Bluff wanted to shout to his assailant to pick on something his own size but thought better of it as it might be good for 'Cocky' to be taken down a peg or two. The fight was soon finished and the excitement cooled down and then a different noise could be heard - the sound of engines arriving. Bruce looked out and saw the people who worked in the Sanctuary and had to giggle because those who came on machines with two wheels had great big round objects on their heads which made them look entirely different.

"Is Susan there amongst them?" enquired Bluff.

"How the dickens should I know" said Bruce "you can't tell. They have all got strange hats on their heads!"

The rain was easing off now and more animals appeared on the lawns. "I must find out from Cocky what they are called" thought Bluff "because you can't go around saying they are 'chicken things' forever."

Some of the animals out there looked really weird and Bobby kept his head inside just in case they were not too friendly. The noises they made were odd but none of them really came close to the stable block.

"Breakfast" cooed Susan as she came into the stalls. Don was given a hay net and so was Bluff but the two greys received hot bran, mixed with sugar beet pulp plus a net and the aroma from their breakfast nearly drove Don to distraction.

"Who wants a hay net after smelling that" grumbled Don. Nevertheless he started to tuck in immediately. Bluff hoped that after breakfast the girl would let them out to the paddocks. He rather liked the grass in this part of the world and the thought of munching it made him rather excited. A loud shout made the ponies rush to the doors of their stables and there, as large as life, was a big animal lorry - just like the one that had brought them there. It was being backed across the lawns towards the stable block.

"They're not shifting us again, are they?" cried Bruce to Bluff.

"I hope not" replied Bluff "I shall refuse to go!"

"And me" called out Don "even if that slip of a girl is trying to starve me to death. I won't budge!" Bobby decided not to look and went to the back of the stall.

The lorry turned and backed past the block out of sight.

"What on earth are they doing?" enquired Bruce. "I've just seen Old Portly and Susan with the lorry plus a right scruffy fellow!"

"What do you mean - scruffy?" asked Bluff.

"You know, like a pitman before he has had a bath" went on Bruce.

"I wonder if they're bringing more ponies here to join us?" said Bluff.

"Where would they put them? There is only one stable block and we live in that!" replied Bruce.

"Perhaps they've brought in some other animals then" went on Bluff. "No doubt we'll soon see."

After a while the lorry left and Susan came to the stalls. "Bruce and Bobby can go out with Bluff for an hour. Don can join them later for half an hour" she announced.

"Half an hour" thought Don "that is disgraceful. This girl is deliberately picking on me for no reason."

The greys and Bluff were taken out of the stalls and into the paddocks. The reason for the arrival earlier of the animal lorry then became apparent. All three ponies stopped and refused to move for out there in the paddocks were three of the ugliest animals they had ever seen. They were larger than the ponies with large stick-like objects poking out of their heads. Bluff stiffened his front feet and raised his head. "No way am I going out there, I would rather starve" he said to himself. The greys lunged at the thought of going anywhere near those creatures.

"Don't be silly" said Susan "they are only cows."

"COWS" thought Bluff "What are they? They look fierce

- I'm certainly not going out there."

Susan asked one of her colleagues to drive the cows across the field and the three ponies were gently edged into the paddock.

Instead of having their usual 'freedom' gallop, all of them bunched up and kept a wary eye on the beasts across the field. Suddenly, the cows saw the ponies and with a swift run (it certainly was not a gallop), they came towards them. Bluff was the first to see them and with panic in his voice cried "Run for your lives!" Without more ado, all three ponies raced off in the opposite direction with three cows in hot pursuit. "Don't stop" called Bobby as he led the stampede. "Don't worry" cried Bluff "we're right behind you" and the thunder of hooves echoed across the paddocks bringing out all the staff to have a look.

Soon it was Don's chance to enter the paddock and when the cows saw him, they stopped chasing the others and made a bee-line for him. With rear hooves kicking and in full and flowing gallop, the black pony headed for his friends who, for their part, were calling out: "Clear off, Don. Don't come near us!"

"That's nice" thought Don as he tried to manoeuvre for all he was worth "What on earth are these things" he wondered as his little legs rushed him over the turf at a fair rate of knots. One thing was certain, they were not ponies.

After a while, the cows gave up the chase and all the animals stopped and stood with their flanks heaving. It was a good few minutes before even Don got down to the task of eating. Bluff grumbled about his age and declared that he must have lost quite a few pounds in those last minutes. He declared that never again would he run from them! "What will you do then?" asked Bobby, who was making a point of keeping himself positioned with Bruce between him and the cows.

"I shall stand and fight!" replied Bluff.

"Maybe they don't want to fight" said Bruce through a mouthful of grass.

"Then I shall tell them to clear off and not bother us" retorted Bluff.

"'ere, 'ere" chirped Bobby.

By this time Don had caught up with his friends and they told him that those "things" were cows, which was of little interest to Don who was busily filling himself with goodness.

"My, you did kick out well!" said Bobby.

"Kick out well!" spat Don "which three cowards told me to keep away then?"

"Well, that was in the heat of the moment" replied Bobby.

It must be said, with the exception of Don, that all the ponies were glad when Susan, assisted by one of the staff, came out to bring them in. Don made a run for it and to the amusement of Susan and her colleague, ran straight towards the cows, who, by this time, were ready for another chase. Poor Don ran for all he was worth and with no other pony to help, felt very much alone. "Why did I have to run?" he thought. "I wish I'd gone in with the others." He rushed towards the gate and as he reached it, only feet in front of his pursuers, Susan arrived. The cows veered off and Don was saved. He felt he would never be able to thank Susan enough and vowed that he would not run off again - well- not until tomorrow anyhow! He was led back to the stables and saw his friends hitched to a rail. Bluff then told him the bad news. All the ponies still had too much coal dust in their coats and today was the day when Susan was to get it out. It would appear that coal dust made the poor girl sneeze and Old

Portly had decided that the sooner the dust was taken away from their coats, the better. Bluff made a note that Susan was not as tough as Ivor or the other pitmen. They never sneezed much with the dust. He wondered "Maybe this is the reason that the people here talk so strange.... It may have something to do with it!"

Bluff had to concede that Ivor was not so pleasant to look at as Susan and he never smelt as nice either; but there again, Susan never gave them any bread and cheese. "Maybe she doesn't eat" he thought and his mouth watered thinking of the bread and cheese. The hitching rail was a hive of industry as Susan and three of her colleagues worked hard to remove the dust from their coats, with Old Portly hovering in the background, giving orders. He sounded very much like the supervisors in the pit who were always shooting their mouths off, although Bluff remembered his deputy very well - he was a nice man.

"Look up" said Don "here comes trouble."

The ponies looked round and there was Mr. Harry, the vet, complete with little bag and eye glass. All the ponies were ready to count how many times the glass fell out but that was soon forgotten when Mr. Harry prepared four enormous syringes. He advanced on Bruce, smacked him on the rump and "hey presto" before Bruce could say "Oh", it was over. Next was Don who managed to get in an "Oh", then Bobby who whimpered "Ooh" before Mr. Harry even touched him. Lastly, Bluff himself who made no sound and with a tear in his eye, proclaimed that he had not even felt it.

"That's their tetanus jab" said the vet. "I'll leave the 'flu one for the next visit. Don't forget to worm them", he said to Susan as he proceeded to examine them.

"Don't you dare come near me" murmured Don "I have

had enough of your insults about being fat."

Nevertheless, Mr. Harry looked down his throat, at his teeth and in his ears.

"Clear off" cried Don but Mr. Harry could not understand him. He gave him a hearty slap on the rump just where the needle had been inserted.

"You torturer" exclaimed the small black pony and moved round sharply.

"I would like my wife to see these ponies" said the vet to Susan, as he moved on to Bruce. "So she can persecute us as well" thought Bluff. All the ponies, including Bobby, stood still for the vet and Bluff mentioned that there was no doubt that this vet knew all about ponies. A remark which drew a rude sound from Don who could not agree. His bottom was still sore. The cleaning was going well and Mr. Harry commented on how the ponies coats were improving by the minute.

"Why don't you go and torture some other poor unsuspecting animal!" Don threw at him.

"Oh, shut up Don" cried Bluff "this vet is really interested in our welfare. After all, he's only doing his job."

"Only because he can't do another" snapped Don and snorted his disgust at Bluff.

Whilst they had been outside, all their stalls had been cleaned and new peat put on the floors. They looked around and felt very proud of their new homes.

"Did you see what they have put on the doors?" asked Bobby.

"No" was the chorus.

"Well, do you remember when we had our photographs taken in our working gear and Bluff stood on the man's foot?

"Oh yes" said Bluff "I remember."

"Well" went on Bobby "those pictures are on each door with our names."

"Get away" said Bruce, feeling annoyed that he had not spotted them first.

"Yes, and they really look like us" continued Bobby.

"Of course they do" retorted Bluff angrily " they ARE us!"

All the ponies craned their necks over the doors to have a look but they were unable to see anything. Don could not get his head over the door at all and bemoaned his lack of inches.

Susan came bustling down to the stables half way through the day and said that the greys could have another hour out in the paddock and after looking at Bluff's stomach, she said that he too could have a break. This really pleased the three ponies because there was nothing they liked better than running loose in the fields. Don came to the door and felt as though his world had caved in. "Why can't they let me out into the field too" he asked himself "why must I always be the odd one out. It just isn't fair."

A few minutes later, Susan appeared with a halter. "Come on, silly" she said "you may not be able to go into the field but there is nothing to stop me from taking you for a long walk." Don could not get the halter on quickly enough. "At least" he thought "I will be able to grab a few mouthfuls of grass as we walk. Can't be bad, can it!"

Susan walked him through the Sanctuary and up the long drive to the lane where they started to walk further. It was really superb! Don grabbed a mouthful here and a mouthful there and in between really enjoyed himself. It was over all too soon but he did appreciate the walk. After all, it was not much fun to be left in the stables all on his own. He began to wonder how the others had fared.

He would have laughed had he known at the time but the

cows had not left them alone for one moment and all three ponies had galloped nearly non-stop. Poor Bluff blew with all the unexpected exertion and the greys were sure they were losing weight by the minute. It really was a nightmare venture and they were absolutely miserable. The three of them wished that they had stayed in the stables with Don. (Little did they know!)

They were all more than glad to see Susan with her helper coming to collect them and even Bobby nosed up to the girl in gratitude. Susan laughed and called them babies for running away from three elderly cows but as Bluff said later, he didn't care for the sharp bits sticking out of their heads! When they found out that Don had been out for a walk with Susan, there were ructions. Bluff declared that it had all been arranged and that Susan had planned the awful chase and had kept Don away from it. A remark which brought a few snorts when Bluff added "... because he was too fat!"

"Nonsense" bellowed Don "I am as trim as a filly" a comment which brought a few snorts from the others. By the time tea was served most of the anger had left the greys and Bluff, and when they were given hot bran and beet mash, their hearts melted towards the girl completely. Even Don was thrilled. He had been given a portion of hot bran with his hay and was well pleased.

As soon as tea was finished and Susan had cleared away the buckets, there was a fluttering of wings and on to Bluff's door flew Cocky Bantam.

"Watcha ugly" he called to Bluff.

"Will you stop calling me that!" snapped Bluff.

"Why?" enquired the Bantam.

"It's not nice" retorted Bluff "and anyhow, I want to have a word with you about the hours you keep."

"What's wrong with the hours I keep?" asked the bantam.

"Well you get up far too early for us" replied Bluff.

"And remember, we are retired ponies" called out Bruce.

"What's retired?" queried the bantam.

"Never mind" interjected Bluff "we want to make a deal with you."

"What kind of deal?" queried the bantam with a hint of mistrust creeping into his voice.

"Well" went on Bluff "if you leave the stables quietly in the mornings without waking us up, then we will treat you nicely."

"Treat me nicely?" declared Cocky Bantam "I don't care if you treat me nicely or not, that's not a deal! I have a better proposition to make."

"What's that?" enquired Bluff.

"Well it's like this" whispered the bantam "there's a little lady bantam over there who is rather unhappy about where she is staying and if you lot would consider that maybe she could live over here, then that would be what you call a deal."

"Certainly not" spat Bluff "we would never think of such a thing."

"Hang on, hang on" pleaded the bantam "I don't mean with me in this stall, I mean in with fatty or the other two."

"Who are you calling fatty?" cried out Don with a certain amount of hurt in his voice.

"Oh be quiet" snapped Bluff, racking his brains to see where the crafty little bantam had caught him. "What do you others think?" he called.

"It's alright by me" said Bruce "as long as I get my sleep in the mornings."

"And me..." echoed Bobby.

"Tell him to buzz off with his lady friends" called Don, still hurt from Cocky Bantam's remarks on his size.

"Well" continued Bluff "if we said she could use the stall with the greys and leave quietly in the mornings with you, how about that?"

"First class" remarked the bantam "can I go and get her?"

"Well, er, I suppose so" said Bluff and with that there was a whirl of wings and off shot the bantam, clucking to his heart's content.

"I hope we've done the right thing" murmured Bluff after he had gone.

"WE?" argued Don "I don't remember saying I agreed to such a lunatic arrangement."

"Well, we did" rejoined the greys "and three out of four is enough."

"I still think he is devious" said Bluff.

"Well we will just have to see how it goes" went on Bruce, sticking up for the Cream Dun "you've done your best and if we get our rest in the mornings, it will have been worth it."

Bluff felt better for that piece of support and waited for the return of their lodgers.

The nights drew in quickly at that time of year and within seconds Cocky was back with a sweet little lady bantam who, as arranged, flew into the stall where the greys lived.

"Ta mate" Cocky said to Bluff "you're a real nice fellow. "

"Thank you, and make sure you are as well" replied Bluff.

"Goodnight darling" shouted the bantam to his sweetheart. "Goodnight love" was the reply and the ponies had a job not to laugh.

"I'd like you to tell us about the animals who live here" said Bluff to Cocky.

"Especially that big one who gave you a right tousing!" interjected Don.

"Gave me a right tousing?" continued the bantam "he was sorry he crossed my path, I can tell you!"

"It didn't seem that way to us!" said Bruce.

"Oh, you must have seen the thing when he caught me a lucky blow" replied Cocky. "As for the other animals that live here.... Well, there are us bantams who are the prettiest ones by far, then there are some hens they saved from being made into pies, an ancient turkey who has seen better days and a couple of ducks and geese. There's a whole flock of other flying birds and a load of cats - all past it of course! Oh yes, I was forgetting, and some dogs - they belong to the geezer who runs the place. The funny thing is though, apart from us bantams, all the other inmates are old and decrepit!"

"Now just you hang on a minute" interrupted Bluff "I think you're being rude."

"Why, because you are all old?" asked Cocky.

"We're not as old as you make out" snapped Bluff and his condemnation of the bantam was endorsed by the greys and Don who swore he would literally kick the bantam out of the stables when the chance arose.

"Aren't you a thin skinned lot!" sneered Cocky "you've no sense of humour at all, have you?"

A little voice chirped from the rafters: "Please let me get some sleep."

"Belt up!" snapped Don.

"Now watch it!" said Cocky, all eager to defend his lady's honour.

The rest of the evening was passed quietly mostly due to the hard galloping that the three had experienced that day. Bluff decided that cows should be banned from the Sanctuary.

Ponies always enjoy a good sleep and it seemed that they

could re-live the many adventures they had experienced that day. It must have been very late when Portly and his confounded light came round the stables amid murmurs of "clear off" and "turn that rotten light off" from the ponies. Give him his due, Old Portly always shouted a cheery "goodnight lads" as he made off to his house across the green.

Bluff decided that he would lay down on the warm peat. He was so comfortable, he decided to stretch. Don preferred to stand and lower his head and enjoy his snooze. The greys lay down and the stables were left in silence which was broken by the odd cackle from Cocky Bantam as he dreamed his dreams.

Chapter 6

Stuck Fast

It was quite late when Bluff awoke. He looked up and, true to his word, Cocky Bantam had left quietly. He decided to get up, but, oh dear! He had moved too close to the corner and was trapped! He could not move.

"Help!" he shouted, and his cries awoke the other ponies.

"What's up with you now!" called Don.

"I'm stuck, you fool!" cried Bluff.

"How do you mean? Trapped?" asked Bruce.

"I can't get up!" replied Bluff "I am too close to the wall!"

"Does it hurt?" enquired Don.

"No it doesn't" snapped Bluff "It's just that I can't move."

"Well you will just have to wait for Susan to come and rescue you then, won't you!" retorted Don and Bluff noticed the hint of sarcasm in his voice.

"It's all right for you" he went on "you're not the one who's stuck!"

"Well, if it doesn't hurt then it won't matter if you wait for the young lady to assist you, will it" sneered Don.

Bluff felt such a fool. Would he ever live it down that he was stuck in his stall! He hoped all the other animals would not get to hear about it, especially THAT bantam. HE would have a field day.

Soon Bluff heard the strange noises as the machines, on which the staff came to work, arrived. He knew that Susan would come down to the stables almost at once. It was a habit with her.

"Oh, do hurry up" he thought "I am getting cramp lying here." It seemed ages before he heard her voice saying "Good morning boys" and then the exclamation "Why, poor old Bluff. What are you doing.." There was no doubt about it. The girl knew her job. She had obviously encountered problems like this before and with a shout to one of the staff who was passing the stables to help her, she started to move the pony, who by his own reckoning, was no mean weight. Bluff felt very self conscious about his predicament and was most anxious to be extricated from it.

The relief when she said "Come on now, you can get up!" Bluff could feel the pins and needles in his legs and his movements were more like a drunken pony than an "old war horse" of some twenty five years. Susan gave him a quick rub down to get the circulation going and then set about providing breakfast.

"Are you all right?" enquired Bruce.

"I think so" returned Bluff "just a little bit shaken up, that's all."

"You're putting it on" quipped Don, who by this time was getting impatient for his breakfast.

"That's the trouble with you" retorted Bluff "you have no feelings for others."

"Not when I'm hungry" was the reply.

In all the confusion, none of the ponies had ventured to notice the weather outside and it was Bobby who remarked on the glorious Autumn day. To a pit pony who has worked underground all his life, every day is a glorious day but some are more glorious than others - and this was one them. The sun shone and with the leaves on the trees in their russet shades, it really was something to behold. Bluff felt better.

Looking forward to his break in the paddock, he only hoped that those wretched cows would leave him alone. Don complained to the two greys about the noise they made when they ate their beet pulp.

"How can we help it" asked Bruce.

"Well, you needn't make so much noise munching it" replied Don. "Especially when you know that I don't get any!"

"Oh, I see" said Bruce "you're jealous!!"

"No, just greedy!" interjected Bluff.

As soon as they had finished feeding, Susan came to take the three out to the paddocks and to their joy, she had shut the infernal cows in one of the paddocks and left the other empty for them.

"Good old Susan" cried Bruce as he kicked and bucked around the field.

"Hear, hear" echoed Bluff, emulating Bruce but definitely kicking higher.

Bobby was content just to gallop and he loved to feel the air rushing by his head and his mane flowing as he went.

The stupid cows were running up and down the dividing fence, kicking and bucking like the ponies.

"I think they're poking fun at us" commented Bruce.

"Oh, just ignore them" said Bluff and he galloped away as fast as his little legs would take him.

Don meantime was tethered outside his stall whilst Susan was cleaning it. Every time she passed him, she gave him a pat.

"You won't get round me that way" thought Don.

"The farrier is coming today." Don peered around and saw Old Portly talking to Susan.

"Ask him to put lightweight shoes on Don's front feet" he

said and Susan nodded and carried on cleaning. Old Portly, looking as important as he could, walked away.

It is well known that farriers and ponies get on very well together, mainly because the latter enjoy having their feet trimmed and also a farrier is very sure-handed which ponies like. It was with some pleasure to Don, therefore, to know that his feet were going to be attended to and he knew the others would equally welcome the news. Susan came over. "Come on fatty" she said smiling "time for your trip to the field."

"Don't you start on about my weight" thought Don as he trotted beside her to the field, his mouth watering as he neared the paddock. "Stop slobbering" cried Susan, wiping her hand on her overall. She opened the gate, took him in and like a shot out of a cannon, he ripped across the field towards his friends. Just as he anticipated, they were all pleased to hear that their feet were going to be examined and from the looks of their hooves, they needed attention!

All too soon, it was back to the stables but not before a struggle had taken place. With the cows out of the way, every one of the ponies played the girl up and she had to run all over the field. One of Susan's colleagues came along holding an apple but she was no more successful than Susan. Bluff was the first to give up. Then Bruce and when he had gone Bobby always followed. Only Don remained - and could he run! BUT he would not run too far in case Susan left him out on his own. OR, what could be worse, if she let the cows back into the field. So his protest about being taken back to the stables was only token. He was too crafty to overplay his hand. Besides, Susan was not beyond giving him a dig in the ribs.

"A quick snooze before the farrier comes" thought Don, as he stood in his stall and with that he dropped his head and dozed off. Bluff, on the other hand, preferred to look out of the stall, over the door to see what was going on. The greys too had their heads over their door. The place was full of animals and although Bantam had told them about the types of animals which lived there, none of them had a clue what they were looking at.

"There's Cocky Bantam and his girl friend over there" said Bobby and the other ponies looked over to where the two bantams were busily pecking at something or other on the grass. Cocky looked up and saw the ponies. "What? Have you just woken up then?" he sniggered sarcastically.

"Don't answer him" said Bluff and looked away. "Why does he have to be so rude every time he sees us?" wondered Bluff.

It was a superb day and for the time of year, quite warm. In fact, it was warm enough to make Bluff sleepy and he went to the back of the stall to have a nod.

Mr. Parkin, the farrier, was a short, muscular man and was one of the 'old school' as far as horses went. He loved them and his caring showed through his rough exterior. "Which'n shall us 'ave fust Miss?" he asked Susan.

"Would you like Don first?"

"Nah. Think oi'll leave 'im 'till last" replied Parkin. "Any of t'other three'll do."

With that Susan tethered Bluff. In fact, when she went to get him he woke with a start. "Must be getting deaf" he mused, looking a little sheepishly at Susan as she placed his halter on his head. Whenever Bluff had his feet attended to, it was like a little bit of heaven to him and he stood as quietly as he could and then nodded off. Looking round and seeing the rear of the farrier presented to him caused him to smile inwardly at the thought of Susan leaping into the air. He wondered how her bruise was now, although he had not seen her limping lately. Both Bruce and Bobby stood for the man as he trimmed their feet.

When it came to Don, it was a different story. Although he had worn shoes on his feet before, the feeling of having his hooves hammered upset him quite a bit. He would not hold still, in fact, he almost came close to panic and that was strange for Don. The farrier was a most patient man and his soft voice helped to calm the worried pony. He asked Susan to hold Don's head and of course, that gave licence for the pony to try and nip her which in turn caused her to box his ear. He then started to nod his head up and down, causing the farrier to lose the leg. It took ages for the shoes to be fitted and at the end of it the farrier asked Susan to walk "the little devil" up and down for him. Don had to admit that he felt better on his feet than he had for many a year. "When 'e loses some weight 'e'll be able to go without shows agin!" said Mr. Parkin as he cleared up his tools and packed them away. Don was so upset. "Even the farrier is weight mad" he thought. "Why don't they just starve me and be done with it!"

The days at this time of year were very short and it was not long after the farrier had gone when Cocky Bantam and his girl friend fluttered up on to the door.

"Didn't hear us go this morning, did you!" he said "like mice we were and there was you, old horse, snoring your head off."

"I do not snore" retorted Bluff, rather annoyed that this little creature was once again having a go at him.

"Don't snore?" was the reply "you don't only snore but you talk in your sleep as well. Maybe you don't talk ... but you don't half make a row!"

"Let me tell you" argued Bluff "I am a very quiet sleeper!"

"You're joking" returned Cocky. "Anyhow, I've got some news for you. We heard Old Portly saying to that girl who looks after you that the Captain wants a welcoming ceremony, whatever that is, for you lot soon."

"He can't be serious" interjected Bruce "we had one of those before we left the pits."

"Well, you've got another one coming up then" went on Bantam "only this is to be very big. He told that girl that we would all have to be locked up that day, so me and my girlfriend here are going to hide!"

"I can't understand why they want another one of those things" said Bobby "why can't they just let us get used to this place and settle down."

"That's not all" crowed Bantam "I heard that some of you are going to a place called London to be put on something called 'television.'"

"What on earth is that?" asked Bluff.

"How do I know?" replied the bantam "I only tell you what I hear, and that's what I hear."

"Must be another farm" said Bruce.

"Oh, he's just lying as usual" snapped Don, stamping his feet.

"I am not lying" protested Bantam "it has upset all the other animals knowing that they will have to be shut up for a day because of you lot!"

"Because of us?" growled Don "we don't want any of the silly fuss. We are supposed to be retired from work and enjoying ourselves."

"Well, we are really" soothed Bobby.

"We are, my hind hoof!" exploded Don. "Take me for example. I'm told by everyone I meet that I am too fat! I'm stopped from going out in the fields, except for a measly 'time.' I have walks with a slip of a girl and you tell me I am **enjoying** it?" The anger welled up inside him. Don knew that this outburst had been building up for a long time and maybe he would feel better now he was getting it off his chest. All the other ponies knew exactly what he was going through and in their hearts, they also realised that the people were only doing it for Don's sake. Bluff had an idea that if they did not look after their old friend, then he might not last all that long and Bluff dreaded anything happening to "fatty."

"You see, Don" said Bruce "when you retire it takes a long time to settle down to the different life. You can't expect miracles, and humans like to fuss about things and we are the things they like to fuss about!"

"Rubbish" replied Don, although in his heart he knew that Bruce was right.

The greys were glad when Susan brought the tea around. It was an ideal time to break up the rather nasty argument. She looked up into the rafters and saw the bantam.

"And you can come down!" she said to him, prodding him with the blunt end of a hay fork. Poor old Bantam had a job holding his balance.

"Clear off, you vicious thing!" he cackled. "You'll break my flipping neck" but she still kept prodding until she finally dislodged him.

"I hate you" he squawked. "Why don't you mind your own business..." but it was no good. She bundled him under her arm and took him out.

"I wonder why she did that?" enquired Bobby. A little voice in his stall piped up: "The man who runs the Sanctuary likes all of us to be locked up at night in a special house. He is afraid the foxes may get us."

"It would have to be a blooming big fox to get you up there" pointed out Bruce.

"I know," said the hen "they do this from time to time. He'll be back tomorrow night."

Secretly Bluff was pleased to see Cocky Bantum have his feathers ruffled a bit and when Susan came back to clear the buckets and wish them all a cheery "goodnight" Bluff nudged her with his nose as if to say "well done." He noted that the hen kept very quiet in the next stall.

"What are foxes?" enquired Bobby.

"I don't know really" replied the hen "but they say that some of our relatives were eaten by them!"

"Ugh" said Bobby "fancy eating something like you, ugh!" Bluff tried to change the conversation by asking how their feet were and all four agreed that they felt really comfortable. Suddenly Bruce came up with a wonderful piece of deduction. "You know these people wear strange things on their heads when they come to work" he said "I have thought out what it reminds me of."

"What?" asked Bobby.

"Pitmen's helmets" replied Bruce "only much bigger.

"No" protested Bobby "pitmen never wore their hats going home - they only wore them at work."

"That's it" exclaimed Bruce "people here do things the other way around.."

"I know they talk and act different from the pitmen" reasoned Bobby "but not that different surely!"

"You have to admit" went on Bruce "they don't even swear like the pitmen!"

"Oh, no" returned Bobby. " I have never heard Susan come out with any of the words that the miners used!"

Bluff was completely lost by this conversation and decided that the best thing he could do was to go to the back of the stall, hang his head and doze off. He was absolutely sure that he would not lie down tonight. Don continued to forage around the stall as he usually did in the evenings, and on finding nothing he too went to the back and hung his head. The two greys decided to have a game before settling down and they chased each other round the stall. When Bruce accidentally kicked Bobby that put an end to the fun and they both stretched out in the warm peat for the night.

The life style for the four old ponies had changed so much since leaving the pits that every night, at some time, their dreams took them back to the days when they worked very hard. What wonderful stories they could tell of those times. When Old Portly came around last thing that night he did not say a word - he did not want to disturb the reveries of the ponies.

Chapter 7

Daily Routine

Bruce was the first to awaken and went to lean over his door. He was taken aback by the white frost that covered the grass and gardens. He stepped back and said to Bobby:

"That's the coldest it has been since we arrived. You should look out there.." Bobby went over and he too was surprised because in the stables where they used to live, they could usually feel the frost coming down during the night. Their present quarters, however, were so well insulated they had not even noticed a change in the temperature.

Bluff was somewhat slow in looking out. He never liked the cold and Don decided to let the outside warm up a bit before he would go to the door. They could hear Old Portly whistling his dogs and knew it would not be long before the rest of the people arrived.

Bobby maintained that once his nose grew used to the cold, it was nice looking out at all the patterns the frost made. "After all" he said "it is a lovely day with bright sunshine and already where the sun shines, the white is going." He heard the familiar sound. "They're here!" he shouted excitedly as he heard the pop, pop, pop of the machines arriving, although from the stables, he could not make out who it was. Bruce pushed in beside him and whinnied "It is always wise to let them know you're about" he thought. His whinny brought Bluff up to the door and his greeting was masked by a bit of a shiver. "The blood must be getting thin" he told himself.

Don was not bothered. He really could not bring himself to get excited over the girl; she did nothing much for him and the way the others were carrying on, they sounded like lovesick fillies.

"Good morning boys" called Susan as she came to the stables. "I hope you are all well this morning."

"Well we might be" retorted Don "we're starving too."

His outburst made no sense to Bluff who was too engrossed in watching Susan.

"As it's so cold today, I am going to give you all hot bran with pony nuts and your hay net. What do you think about that?" she asked and this was met with instant approval by all.

"Why don't you get on with it, instead of yakking on..." shouted Don who by now was listening to the noises his stomach was making. "I swear that one day I will collapse" he moaned.

"You are ungrateful" called out Bruce "you are never satisfied with anything this girl does for you. You were the same down the pit. No wonder Charlie took to betting! He must have been sick and tired of your perpetual complaining!"

"Look mate" snapped Don "I happen to be flipping hungry. I also happen to get fed up with this biddy and her yap, yap, yapping, so if you don't like it you can do the other thing!"

By this time Don had succeeded in upsetting all the ponies and they stood very quietly and waited. Susan had put some crystals in each bucket of bran as well as pony nuts; she was worming them without them knowing. She smiled and thought "I can be as devious as you lot when I like." She entered Don's stall. She had heard a lot of noise going on in the stables and did not realise that it was about her the ponies were arguing. All she knew was that when she took the food around, she was met by silence. The smell of the buckets brought them to life however and all that could be heard coming from the three stalls was the grinding of teeth.

With breakfast over and the frost fast disappearing from the grass, Susan came back to collect the empties. She always gave the ponies a pat as she came into the stall and as Bluff had a habit of nuzzling her as she passed, she often put her arms around his neck and gave him a hug which he liked.

"I've got some news for you four" she said. "They are going to have a welcoming ceremony for you and all the people from the village have been invited to come and see their special guests."

"So Cocky was right then" murmured Don after she had gone. "They are going to mess us around again."

"You really have got to get used to it" returned Bluff "people like doing these things. Besides, if the village people come down, then no doubt they will bring lots of bits and pieces for us like sugar lumps and carrots."

"And apples" added Bruce.

"Yes, and apples" returned Bluff carrying on " so you see, Don, it might be good for us too."

"Well, if you put it like that.." replied Don "it might be worth it. But I am not too keen on these people making such a fuss."

Susan did not appear to mind. She seemed very happy as she came to collect them to lead them to the paddocks. As usual, the cows had a lot to say for themselves and the names they called the ponies were most uncomplimentary. They upset Don by calling him "Squirt" and Bluff by referring to him as "Shorthouse." The greys got away without being called anything.

The vet was waiting for Susan when she returned from putting the ponies out. They greeted each other.

"How are your old chums this morning?" asked Mr. Harry.

"Oh, they're all right" she replied "although I was wondering though if you had noticed that the greys seem to be losing weight, especially Bobby. I've wormed them this morning but I must admit I'm a little concerned."

"I wouldn't worry too much" answered the vet "after all, it's early days for them yet. How's Don taking to his diet?"

"He isn't" she said "I have the distinct feeling that he resents me not feeding him."

"He's a crafty little beggar" Mr. Harry remarked "and he will try every trick in the trade to get more food. Talking about food, I think it will be all right if they stay on grass for the whole morning from now on. There's not a lot of goodness in it and I would say Don can stay with them, but make his hay net just a little smaller."

"Thank you, Mr. Harry" said Susan. The vet walked down to the paddocks to have a look at the ponies. He was already very fond of these four and he felt very proud that they could rest in the luxury of the Sanctuary. The ponies were all busily grazing and to the outsider, it would appear that they had not seen the vet but it was Don who muttered: "Don't look up now but trouble is at the gate!" The others swivelled their eyes without lifting their heads to see whom he meant. On seeing the vet, they told Don off for saying he was trouble! **THEY** liked Mr. Harry. Later on in the morning Bluff looked around. They seemed to have been out in the field for a long time. He wondered if Susan had forgotten them and mentioned it to the others.

"Don't you dare utter a word" warned Don "let's enjoy

ourselves whilst we can!"

Sauntering towards them, followed closely by about six little hen bantams, was Cocky Bantam himself. "Morning" he called. "Did you miss me last night after that wretched biddy grabbed me?"

"Not really" returned Bluff "although I must admit it was pretty to watch and I knew from the start that she would catch you."

"That stupid girl could have broken my neck!" fumed Cocky.

"Where did she take you?" asked Bobby.

"Oh, there's an old building over by the dung heap where they put us lot" explained Bantam "we are all thrown in together. It's a weird set-up. There are all sorts of broken down old chickens littering the place and you can't get a good night's kip for all the twittering going on."

"But at least you are safe from the fox" interrupted his little bantam lady. Bluff mentioned that Susan had informed them of the ceremony which was coming and Bantam wheeled round on Don and said: "Hey, you, fatty! You owe me an apology for calling me a liar."

"Rubbish." replied Don. "I never asked you what holds your ears apart!" was the sarcastic reply and the bantam had to flutter out of the way pretty sharply when Don ran over to clobber him. It was quite a pretty sight to see the bantam actually flying about five feet off the ground with Don in hot pursuit, shouting: "I'll kick you out of the field if I catch you, you nasty little wretch" and Bantam shouting back: "Go and pick on someone your own size!"

The cows in the other paddock all joined in the uproar and were dashing up and down. Bantam beat Don to the fence, closely followed by his retinue of ladies. Don was absolutely livid with Cocky and when he spotted that the cows were trying to get in on the act, he dashed across the field to have a go at them. To the surprise of all the ponies, as soon as the cows saw Don running towards them, they took to their heels and fled. "They are bloomin' cowards!" cried Bruce who, by this time, had gone across to lend moral support to the small black pony.

"Oh boy, we'll never have to run from them again" chortled Bluff, as Bobby joined the other two.

"Come back and fight!" shouted Don, stamping the ground with frustration and anger.

"Scaredy cows!" cried Bobby. But the cows were over the far side of the field, pretending to be eating. Don felt cheated and galloped across to see if there was another chance of catching the bantam but the wise old bird had taken his leave of the field and disappeared into the Sanctuary. Bluff and the greys ran up to Don in order to calm him down because they could see he was so angry.

"Fancy that little upstart saying that all I had between my ears was rubbish" complained Don "I'll flippin' catch him, honest I will!"

"Now, now, Don "soothed Bluff "it's not worth getting all upset because of a bantam. He is always cheeky, especially to me!"

"And me" chirped up Bobby, not wanting to be left out of the bother that was going on.

After the hectic morning, only token resistance was offered when the girls came to bring the ponies back to the stables. Bobby was the worst but soon surrendered when he thought he was going to be left behind. Bluff really did enjoy his grooming after being out all morning. When Susan bent down to clean his feet, he always turned his head just to see how quickly she could straighten up and threaten him. All the ponies had a groom and clean up before going back into their stalls. Bluff and Don usually went to the back of the stall to hang their heads, which made Susan think they were sulking but they were not. They were just tired. The greys were always active and the conversation that afternoon was about the place where they had come from. They knew that Don was from Shetland (wherever that was) and they had an idea that they were Welsh ponies but it did not mean much to them, except that they were much bigger than their two other friends.

The afternoon was uneventful. All the ponies settled down in their own way but their peace was shattered later on in the day by the flutter of wings in Bluff's doorway.

"Watcha ugly" Bantam crowed.

"Look here" returned Bluff "you've been chased once today and if you're not careful, you'll be chased again!"

"What's wrong with me calling you ugly, ugly?" Bantam enquired.

"Bbbbecause III hhhappen nnot to be wwhat you sssay I am" Bluff stammered, feeling a little embarrassed with the conversation.

"Oh, I don't mean you are really ugly, you know" said Bantam "it's a form of endearment."

"One I could do without" snapped Bluff.

"I hope Susan sees you again tonight" said Bruce "it gave us all great pleasure to see you being bundled out of here last night."

"Yes, you can smirk" grieved Bantam "it wasn't you that was being hurt, was it?"

"Being hurt, my left hoof" rejoined Bluff "she was as gentle as can be with you!"

"That girl is vicious. She should never be let loose on law abiding bantams!"

"Law abiding....! Don't make me laugh" said Bluff. "If you are law abiding, what are you doing over here in the stables when you are supposed to be over there with feathered things of your kind?"

"They smell" announced Cocky Bantam.

"So do you!" said Don with a snort. By this time, the bantam's friend had arrived and quietly settled to roost up in the rafter. Cocky flew up and quite cleverly hid himself behind the main stay. He could not be seen.

"The crafty blighter" thought Bluff.

Chapter 8

Banging a Bucket

The rattle of the buckets meant that tea was on its way and was accompanied by snorts and excitement from all four ponies. Tonight there was hot bran mash with a few pony nuts and beet pulp for the greys, with bran mash and pony nuts for Don and Bluff. It smelt delicious. All heads were deeply immersed in the buckets and had the ponies been cats, they would have purred.

Bluff had all but finished his bran and could see a speck more at the bottom of the bucket so he pushed his head in just a little bit more to get his tongue around the last morsel.. It was as he tried to pull his head out of the bucket that he found it was wedged inside the container. He could not move it.

"Help, help" he cried. "Help!"

"What's up mate?" called Don with a mouthful of moist bran.

"I've got my head stuck in the bucket" moaned Bluff, in a muffled voice.

"You must be joking!" said Bruce.

"I'm not" cried Bluff "it seems as though night has come early."

The ponies could hear the constant clanging as poor Bluff stumbled from wall to wall.

"Cor, that hurt" they heard him say and then BANG!

Bluff was beginning to panic a little and sweat up.

"Oh, why doesn't Susan come" he thought "she'd know

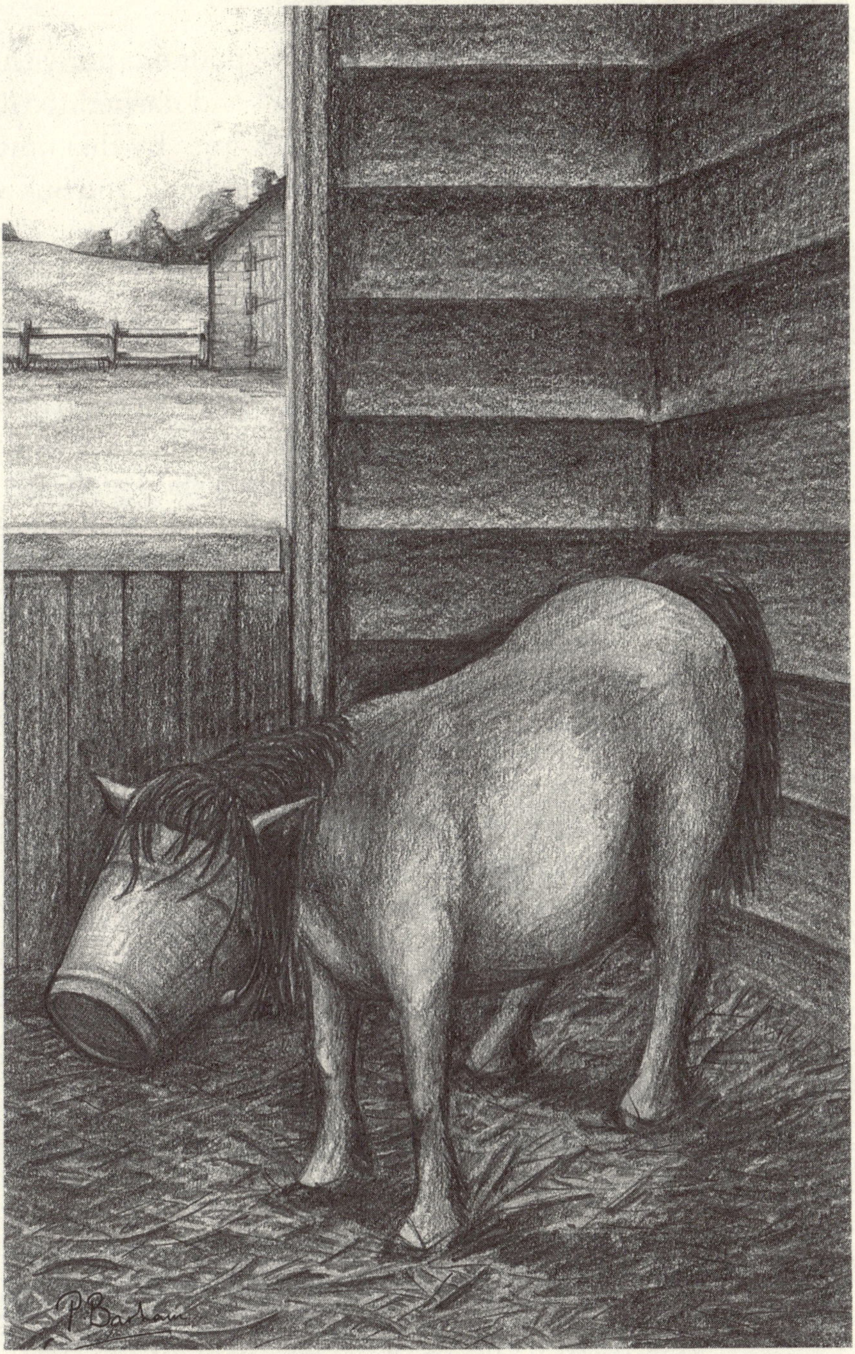
P. Barham

what to do."

Susan did come and when she saw the poor old pony she exclaimed "Bluff, what have you done?" and dashed to the door to call one of the staff who was passing. By this time, Bluff was beginning to grunt and groan with panic and Susan knew she had to work fast.

"I want two or three people here sharp!" she cried as she directed the girl to the office to get help and call the vet. Susan put her arms around Bluff and quietly talked to him. "Steady, old boy" she said "we'll soon get you out of this. Steady, now steady." Her voice was having a soothing effect on the pony and calming him down. He was almost in a state of terror.

Help arrived and together Susan got them to hold Bluff whilst she gently tried to ease the bucket off his head. Bluff did not have the sense to hold still. He again started to become agitated and Susan was having difficulty holding him.

"Oh, where's that vet?" she wailed.

"He'll be here as soon as he can" was the reply.

"I hope so! I really hope so!" sobbed Susan. Poor old Bluff had hit the wall so many times in his frenzy to get the bucket off, that in fact he had hammered it on more with each blow. Susan had to be careful in trying to ease it off because she was afraid she might damage his eyes or nostrils. "Where's the vet?" she called but no one answered because no one knew and her enquiry was only one of emotion.

The other ponies by this time had started to get restless and several staff members had to go in and talk to them. Bobby was the worst. He kept calling to Bluff "Whatever have you done?" but of course, Bluff could not answer. He was too busy trying to keep himself from going berserk. Susan felt a movement and knew that slowly the bucket was easing off.

71

The sweat was pouring off her head as she concentrated on her task. She kept stopping now and then to ease the aches in her wrist where she was delicately holding the bucket. A movement at the doorway indicated that Mr. Harry had arrived. He lost no time in preparing an injection to quieten the pony and was pleased to see that the girls had started to remedy the problem. "This should settle him" he murmured and at the same time, he looked to see how far Susan had progressed in removing the bucket. He seemed content that what she was doing was in fact all that could be done.

"You're a funny old fellow" he said to Bluff. "If it had been him next door (indicating Don) then I would have understood it."

"It's coming now" gasped Susan; her arms were nearly dropping off. She could not remember a time when she felt so tired. Suddenly the bucket was off! Poor old Bluff was shivering and shaking and Mr. Harry gave him another injection to slow down the rapid heart beats that the fright had caused. "I would like someone to stay with him for a while" Mr. Harry instructed "just in case there are any repercussions, although I don't think there will be."

"I'll stay" volunteered Susan "I don't think I could go home until I was sure that he was all right."

Bluff meanwhile was slowing returning to his old self but there was no doubt about it, the event had frightened him. The other ponies had by now returned to normal and they all wanted to know what had happened. Cocky, stuck up in the rafters, just wanted everyone to go. He had found hiding from Susan to be very uncomfortable and the last thing he wanted was for her to look up and find him.

"There's a good boy" Susan said gently patting the old pony on the neck. "I think you were very brave and I love you very much. Although Bluff did not know exactly what the word "love" meant, he liked the sound of it. Mr. Harry packed his medical bag and spoke to Old Portly about Bluff and then he turned to Susan and said: "You have done very well there, my dear. I think by calming him down, you most probably saved him from serious injury. If you should want me, ring me at the surgery. I'll be there until about nine o'clock tonight."

"Thank you, Mr. Harry" replied Susan "but I think he'll be all right now." She gently walked the pony round the stall. He had stopped shaking and was more like his old self.

"Will somebody tell me what has happened" called Don but his enquiry was met with silence so he went back to his hay net. "Blow them all" he thought.

Susan stayed with Bluff for a long time. To Cocky Bantam in the rafters, it seemed like eternity. To make matters worse, he had pins and needles in his legs.

"Flipping girl!" he fumed "she haunts me, she really does."

All the ponies spent a subdued time that evening, not wanting to upset Bluff or break the silence that animals feel when there's trouble.

"Goodnight Bluff" said Susan as she prepared to go "I hope you won't do anything else tonight.." and with a "goodnight" to all the others, away she went.

"Thank the lucky stars for that" crowed Cocky "it's past time for my sleep and I thought that she would never go."

Bluff would have liked to tell him off but he did not really feel up to it. Instead he left it to Don to shout: "Just for once, Cocky do give it a rest" and Bantam to reply: "Please yourself."

And all went quiet. "What a day" thought Bluff as he dozed off and the greys settled themselves down in the peat, not knowing what had really happened, or why.

Up in the rafters, the light cackle of the two little bantams was the only thing that broke the stillness of the night and when Old Portly made his rounds at midnight, all that could be heard was the barking of a fox across the paddocks. None of the ponies even knew that he had been to see that all was well.

Chapter 9

Rainburn and Rodeo

As soon as the dawn broke, the ponies were awake. In fact, they were up and about at the same time as the two bantams were making their start to the day.

"What's up with you lot then?" called Cocky, as he preened himself prior to flying off.

"Why?" enquired Bruce.

"Well, normally you are all in the land of nod when we get up" replied Cocky. "It was only a day or two since old grumpy here made me that fantastic offer!"

"I wish I hadn't now" mumbled Bluff, feeling quite normal after his ordeal of the night before.

"Are you ready dear?" Cocky called to his little hen.

"Not yet" was the reply.

"Well hurry up then" cackled the bantam "or we will be late for the early worms."

The weather was not too bright and the ponies decided that it might rain during the day.

"Why were you awake so early Bluff?" called Bruce.

"I don't know" replied Bluff. "It must be something to do with my accident last night."

"What did you do?" enquired Bobby anxiously.

"Well, it was silly really" explained Bluff. "I was doing what Don next door would do - trying to get the last bit from the bottom of the bucket and before I knew it, my head was stuck inside it."

"Did it hurt much?" asked Bobby.

"No, not really" answered Bluff. "It frightened me though and I must admit I did panic a little."

"You can say that again" chortled Don who was really relishing his old friend's embarrassment.

"Well, it wasn't funny!" snapped Bluff "and I bet you would have created a terrific fuss if it had been you!"

"Me?" went on Don "I would have stood as still as a mouse and waited for her highness to come and rescue me."

"Yes, and I can imagine that" said Bruce joining in the conversation. "You would have raised the roof and the stables would have been pandemonium."

"Hang on a minute" interrupted Don "wasn't it me who put those wretched cows in order after you lot had bolted for your lives?"

"Only by accident" chided Bluff.

"Not by accident at all" snapped Don. "By superior strength!!" and the other ponies laughed enough to make them whinny.

Bruce looked out of his door. He had taken to doing that lately as a way of hurrying Susan up. It seemed to him that if he stood by the door, she came sooner, or at least he thought so. The clouds were thickening up and there was a faint breeze which Bruce smelt as rain on the way.

Suddenly, the pop, pop, pop of the strange machines grew louder and louder until there they were, the staff on whom they all depended. "They're here" called Bruce softly and Bluff and Bobby joined him at the doors in order to await Susan. All the staff waved to them and in return they snorted their welcome. Susan came straight down to the stables before going into her building where she took her strange clothes off and put on her uniform. This morning all she had done was to take off her peculiar hat. She went straight up to Bluff and rubbed his nose and said: "How's my brave boy this morning" and for an answer, Bluff rubbed his nose on her shoulder. She said "good morning" to the greys and gave them a pat and then walked to Don's stall where he stood right at the back. "And how's old misery this morning?" she asked. Don turned his head and pretended she was not there.

As soon as breakfast was over, Susan took them one by one down to the paddock so that they could have a complete break from the stables, just as Mr. Harry had advised. They all had a quick gallop to blow away the cobwebs and then settled down to the important task of browsing through the grass and eating to their heart's content. So busy were they with their preoccupation that they scarcely noticed it was raining, not too hard, but just a light downpour. Ponies are not the type of animal to take cover when it rains - not like those cissy cows in the next paddock, who were already in their shelter. Don commented that perhaps they thought they would melt if they got wet. Nobody came for them so they just carried on and Bruce began to feel sore on his back. He did not say anything. Maybe it would go away but it did not. It became worse and felt as if something was burning him.

The others were all busily grazing so he tried to put it out of his mind, but it would not go. It burnt more and more and became unbearable. He found that the pain made him wander around instead of grazing. The more he walked, the worse it became. He went over to Bobby and asked him if he could see anything on his back. Bobby looked but said he could see nothing wrong so he went up to Bluff. "No" said Bluff "your back looks alright to me." Bruce then thought he might be imagining it so he tried to graze again. But it was no use. He became more and more miserable so he stood and hung his head in the rain. He was not tired but he was in pain.

It was about this time that Susan had walked down to the paddock to see if everything was all right and she noticed Bruce standing in the field. She thought it curious that he should be hanging his head in the rain and decided to wander over and have a look at him. "It's strange" she thought "Bruce has not even looked up at me." All the other ponies had acknowledged the fact that she was there. "Very unlike Bruce as he's always polite" she thought. She reached him and looked round him and immediately she knew that Bruce was in trouble because as she put her hand on his back, he shuddered. Without more ado, she went to get his halter. Bruce sensed that she was going to help him so he slowly made his way to the gate to meet her as she returned. Susan led him into the stall and went to phone Mr. Harry.

"What seems to be the matter with him?" asked Mr. Harry over the telephone; and Susan went on to explain what she had seen. "That sounds like rainburn to me" said Mr. Harry "I'll be right down."

Susan did not do anything to Bruce. She just stood there with him waiting for the vet to arrive. As soon as Mr. Harry looked at Bruce he diagnosed that it certainly was rainburn and continued to tell Susan that grey ponies suffered badly from it. As Bruce had not been weathered for long, there was a likely chance of him getting it. He gave Susan some cream which he said would ease the soreness and told her to keep Bruce inside whilst it rained.

Having treated the grey pony, Mr. Harry and Susan walked round the paddock to check the others who were still heads down and munching away. "Not much wrong with this lot!" he commented. "But whilst I am here, I'll have a look at Bluff to see if he has any ill effects from last night."

Bluff was a little put out by this as it interfered with his grazing and Susan should know better than to allow it! As he said afterwards he thought he was a little rude to the vet but at the time Mr. Harry never noticed anything amiss. He put his stethoscope to Bluff's heart and lungs and turned to Susan and said: "He's as strong as an ox, this old fellow! Not a trace of the trauma he went through last night."

"That's good" beamed Susan "I would hate anything to happen to him. He's such a sweet old thing!"

Susan asked the vet why he had earlier suggested having some cattle in the paddocks with the ponies and he explained that cattle eat and kill a kind of worm which is harmful to ponies or horses.

"How do they get on?" he enquired. "They don't very well!" admitted Susan. "They spend their time chasing each other round the paddocks. That's why I separated them."

"Oh, you don't want to do that" said the vet. "Leave them and they will soon learn to live together" and with that he walked to the gate that separated the two paddocks and opened it.

"Will they come to any harm?" asked Susan. "Of course they won't!" Mr. Harry confirmed. "They will spar around like a couple of boxers but they definitely won't fight as such." They continued walking back to the stables -"I'll just look in on Bruce before I go." They went in to see the grey pony who by this time was looking very miserable.

"Don't worry about this small problem" Mr. Harry assured Susan. "We'll soon have him right" and then he left, leaving Susan and Bruce both looking as though the world was about to end. "You ponies do cause me some worry" murmured Susan and then she decided to throw off her depression and went out to bring the others in.

The sight that met her as she walked down to the paddocks was highly amusing for there, in the middle of the field, were the three ponies standing bunched together like a wagon train in the old westerns and acting the part of the Indians were the three cows going round and round! It looked so comical to her as she watched but to the ponies it was horrific.

"Keep your eye on them!" warned Bluff to Don as they stood back to back.

"Don't worry mate!" declared Don "I'll not let these old ladies get near me!"

"I don't think I will be able to cope if they rush us" cried Bobby.

"Yes you will, old friend" Bluff shouted, hoping that his words of encouragement would lead Bobby to have more confidence.

"They're getting awfully close" wailed Bobby "and I think it's me they are going to charge!"

"No they're not" proclaimed Don "I think it's all a big bluff. Why don't we break out of this circle and rush them?"

"Do you think we ought to?" asked Bobby keeping as close to Bluff as he could.

"Oh, I wish Bruce was here" Bobby muttered. "He would know what to do."

"I have already told you what to do" urged Don. "Rush the blighters."

"But suppose they don't move?" cried Bobby.

"Then we've had it" retorted Bluff impatiently.

Just then, Don looked up and saw Susan standing on the bridge laughing, and was he mad. "Hey you two! Look who's over there laughing at us!" Bluff and Bobby never looked to where Don said Susan was standing. They were too

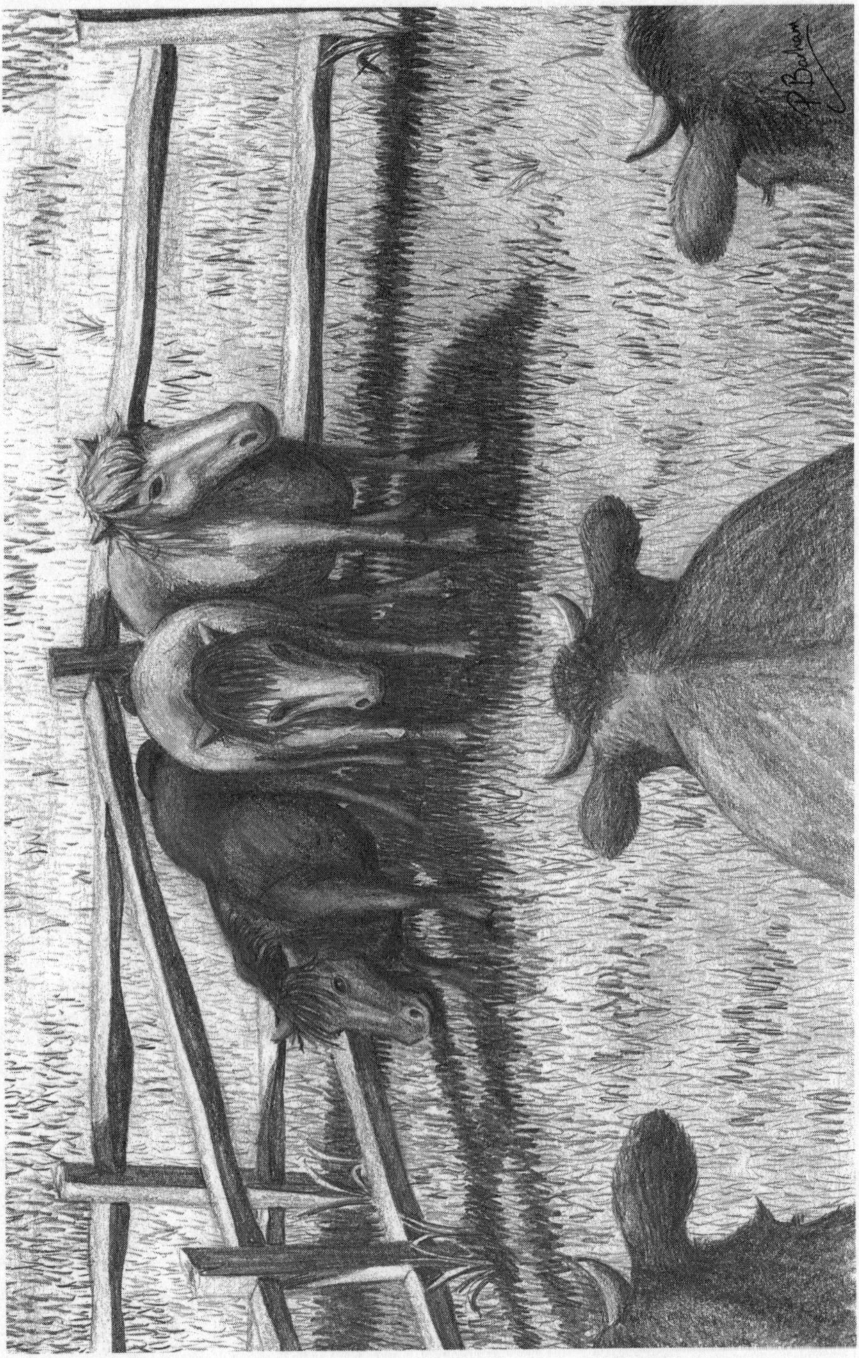

busy keeping a wary eye on the enemy.

"Why doesn't she come and get us?" cried Bobby.

"How the dickens should I know" retorted Don. "It seems to me that she enjoys seeing us in this dreadful situation."

The cows moved and started bellowing.

"We've got to do something soon" said Don.

"Oh dear" whimpered Bobby. "What with the rain and poor old Bruce and now these horrible creatures. What are we going to do?"

"Charge straight at them" shouted Don as he started to prance ready for the off.

The other two ponies were not so sure of success and as Don was smaller than they were, it seemed that his bravado was not all that convincing!

"Look you two" sneered Don "we've got to have this out with these oversized bags of wind, right here and now. I've lost enough time which I should have spent eating!" and he seemed to be getting more and more cross. "If you're going to have a go, then let's have a go now. All right?"

The other two dithered and then Bluff said: "It seems the only thing to do!"

"But I am not too keen," put in Bobby who was slowly getting near to panic.

"All right" said Bluff "let's go" and without thinking, and led by Don who was really angry, the ponies charged. The cows who, taken by surprise, counter attacked. But their resolve was not as strong as the frightened ponies and very soon they gave way and bolted.

It was a real picture, one that Susan would always remember. The ponies bucked and kicked and snorted at the fleeing cows who also bucked and kicked but who in the end out-ran the three brave heroes.

"That will teach them" puffed Don, as he stopped almost out of breath.

"Yeah" replied Bluff, his flanks heaving. Bobby had stopped near the gate and Susan was talking to him. The cows meanwhile were still running.

"My," said Bluff "they must be fit."

"They are a lot younger than us" replied Don who was puffing quite heavily.

"I bet they don't take us on again" volunteered Bluff.

"That's for sure" agreed Don, feeling very proud of himself for having thought of the charge in the first place. Susan, having enjoyed the spectacle, had now started to take the ponies back to the stables but Don resolved that he would get his own back on her for not helping out in the fracas. He decided that she would have to run to catch him today. Little did he know that Susan had no intention of chasing him and was prepared for him to stay out if he liked!

Don did stay for a bit but the cows who now outnumbered him three, to one, were getting a little close and it was time to call for help so he whinnied like mad and ran around the gateway almost pleading to be caught! The more he called, the more he became worried and the closer the cows moved towards him. "Where the dickens is she?" he wondered and whinnied louder. Of course Susan heard him. Everyone in South Bunford heard him! She decided to let him suffer for a little longer. In his frustration he started pushing at the gate but that was no good. He pawed at the ground but to no avail. Poor Don! Would she never come to find him? He started grazing again but the cows ventured closer and closer. He whinnied and at last his call was answered. Susan came down the path. "That will teach you to play me up" she said.

"Play you up" thought Don "you haven't seen anything

yet" and he meekly walked back with her to the stables. Bluff was highly amused at Don's rantings at being left out in the paddock and had Bruce felt better, he most probably would have enjoyed the story. Bobby was too busy fussing around Bruce and trying to comfort him, which in fact made the old grey feel worse.

"What did the vet say was the matter with you?" enquired Bluff.

"Oh, he said it was 'rainburn'" replied Bruce "and they have put some cream on my back which I must say has eased the pain a little. But now I feel I've got it above my eyes!"

"Try to get Susan to notice your head when she comes round the stables" suggested Bobby. All Bruce really wanted to do was to go to the rear of the stall and hang his head. He felt better doing that. He hoped Bobby would not fuss about it too much.

After a while, Susan came to groom them and it was as she was leading Bobby out of the stall, she noticed Bruce was shaking his head and went to have a look. The burn on the pony's head was now noticeable and she tied Bobby up ready to be groomed, and went to get more cream to ease Bruce.

For Don the afternoon dragged. Any time dragged when he was not eating and there was not a lot of chatter in the stables through Bruce being unwell. All Bluff liked doing was snoozing and Don never enjoyed a conversation with Bobby. Susan looked in on a couple of occasions and spent most of her time pampering Bruce, who according to Don, lapped up all the attention. The only time she spoke to Don he turned his head away. HE did not want anything to do with her. HE would never forgive her for not catching him today. Bluff seemed to enjoy the quiet of the afternoon although he could hear Don moaning continuously. He knew it would not be long before his quiet little world would be shattered by the arrival of Cocky Bantam who was bound to remark about Bluff's head getting stuck in a bucket the previous afternoon. It had been another eventful day and they had experienced yet another chapter of their settling-in process. "Teatime!" "Oh those magic words" thought Don. "Hot bran mash, nuts and a sweet, sweet hay net. Paradise! Well, at least until I've eaten it!" Whilst Susan was in the stall with him, he pretended not to be hungry and he convinced her enough for her to say: "Are you sickening for something Don?" to which he would have liked to have said "Yes, you silly girl" but as she would only smile and not understand, he never said it. BUT he had a lot of satisfaction in thinking it.

Bruce perked up with the hot food and Bobby felt better as well. Bluff too would have enjoyed the meal if it had not been for the usual fluttering of wings.

"Hello old Bucket Head!" came the remark.

"Oh, how I hate you" replied Bluff, nearly choking on his food in anger.

"Hate me?" said Bantam, quite surprised. "I can't think why you should. I'm the best mate you'll ever have."

"Best mate!" shrieked Bluff. "You are the, the ... rudest, coarsest, most uneducated animal I have ever seen!"

"I am not an animal actually you know" went on Bantam, knowing that it would add fuel to the fire. "I happen to be of the fowl variety!"

"You're really foul alright" called Don from the next stall.

"Hey" snapped Bantam "when I am talking to the organ grinder, I don't want his monkey to interrupt!"

"I'll monkey you one day" growled Don.

"I don't think I will ever understand you lot" said Bantam in a hurt voice. "I come to see you every night and look forward to passing a friendly word with you. What do I get? Nothing but abuse!"

The ponies could not believe their ears! In all their lives they had never come across a more provocative creature than the cocky little devil sitting up in the roof! AND he had the gall to accuse them of being rude! Even poor old Bruce snorted his disgust at that statement.

Susan came to see to Bruce and then to take away the empty buckets. Bluff nudged her and hoped she would look up and see Cocky Bantam, but no luck. She was intent on giving him a big hug and kiss on the nose.

"Goodnight lads" she cooed "see you in the morning" and away she went.

"Phew, that was close" said Bantam " I thought for one awful moment that you were trying to get her to look up towards me!"

"I was" snorted Bluff.

"Why, you rotten thing!" clucked Cocky. "And you, my best friend."

"Best friend!" hissed Bluff "Why, only a few minutes ago you were accusing me of abusing you and being rude!"

"Oh yes" replied Cocky "friends always abuse each other and are sometimes rude. But never, let me repeat never, do they tell tales on each other!"

"Who's telling tales?" asked the old pony, knowing that he was getting under the bantam's skin.

"I think it's time I got my beauty sleep!" said Cocky, not being drawn into Bluff's trap.

Bluff, in this quiet moment, mused on just what had happened to them since they had moved to this Sanctuary, and, on reflection, he liked it. There had been difficulties, it was true but on balance, there had been victories - and his mind lingered on the cows. Don, though, had behaved quite well and the greys, Bluff thought, were excellent. What of the way they had been treated up to now? Well, Susan was the best they had ever had and although she was fair, she could also be strict with them - as Don had discovered today in the paddock. The vet and the farrier were both first class men and Bluff had a great respect for them both. Of the others in the Sanctuary, he did not know too much about them. Old Portly was really just a voice who came to see them but never interfered with the way they were cared for. "On the whole" considered Bluff "I think the Captain has done us very proud in providing this home" and already he felt that he had lived in the stable block for years. Although he remembered his life in the mines, already the pictures were fading and he was full of the daily routine that was emerging with Susan and the other ponies living with him. Bluff knew that there would be many more adventures whilst they lived there, and the thought of things to come filled him with a tingling feeling in his legs.

Don, in his dreams, was living in a place where food was plentiful and none of the people there looked at all like Susan! THEY were always feeding him and the hay net on his wall was never emptied.

The greys did not dream in the same way as the other two ponies. Bruce and Bobby both waited to see what the morrow would bring.

After the night of dreams, their days continued to be rather unspectacular for many weeks. The important thing that happened was that the ponies gradually became better acquainted with the cows. In an odd way, they all became friendly, although each group stayed in its own territory and fraternization was kept to an absolute minimum.

Cocky Bantam continued his verbal battles with Bluff mostly, but Don inevitably was drawn into the fray and Cocky's hatred of Susan grew as she caught him in the stables more often. Cocky's lady had long since given up the battle to stay and returned to the hen-house. Cocky Bantam was a fighter, however, and his antics became bolder each day. All the ponies had to agree they would be quite lost without the little blighter. Bruce and his rainburn looked very bad for a few weeks but it slowly started to heal, leaving the poor old pony looking as though he had fought a terrifying battle.

Chapter 10

Dress Rehearsal

Day followed day and the weather became steadily worse, making it almost impossible for Bruce to go to the paddock. He had to be content with walks with Susan when it eased up. All the ponies were tired of the rain because it stopped them from enjoying the freedom of the fields that they loved so much. They all knew that preparations were going ahead for their welcoming party because Cocky kept them well informed and they had seen the way Susan and her colleagues kept the place clean and tidy, with extra care being given to the paintwork.

One day, the Captain came to see them and they guessed that the time must be getting close for the 'big day' as they had seen everybody rushing about. Every time the Captain came to see them, he had a habit of looking at their teeth. None of the ponies could understand why but as soon as he saw a pony out of its stall, over he would come and grabbing the muzzle would peer at the poor old thing's teeth which were, to say the least, not all whiteness and brightness. Don thought the man had a thing about teeth and swore that at the first opportunity, he would grab one of his fingers.

Susan came into the stalls one morning and said: "Today, we are going to have a run-through for tomorrow's ceremony, so I want you all to behave and not give me any trouble! Understood?"

"What's a run-through?" enquired Don.

"I don't really know" replied Bluff "but she will show us."

"I don't really want to go anywhere looking like this" moaned Bruce referring to the bald patches on his forehead and back.

"Oh, you'll be fine" assured Bobby "Susan will cover you over in some way, I'm sure."

"I really hope so" said Bruce.

"A lot of nonsense if you ask me" declared Don "We have been here for months and only now the Captain decides to welcome us to his stables. Supposing we don't want 'welcoming' - what then?"

"Do stop it, Don" pleaded Bluff. "You know they want to have a little get-together so that they can tell all the other people what good souls they are for offering us a home."

"Well, I am not going to behave myself!" Don told his friends "so there!"

The previous evening Cocky had perched up on Bluff's door, and started to preen himself ready for the night. "Have you lot heard what they are going to do tomorrow?" he asked.

"We've heard" answered Bluff.

"Well that's all right but when it comes to the real thing, I am going to devise a devilish plan to mess it all up.." went on Cocky with some pride ringing in his voice. "After all, there must be a limit to what us lot will take from that lot."

"I couldn't agree more" called Don from his stall "and I am right with you!"

"Right with me?" chortled the surprised Cocky "I never thought I would see this day!"

"Well, don't get too big headed" snapped Don "it doesn't mean that I like you. It merely means that on this occasion I agree with you - nothing more!"

"What do you plan to do about it?" enquired Cocky with

interest.

"Well, I don't know yet" explained Don "but I'll think of something!"

Bluff was not too sure that messing up the arrangements would be a good thing and asked the greys what they thought. Bobby was all for not doing anything that would upset anybody and Bruce felt that the sooner it was over the better. Cocky Bantam thought that both the greys were a little soft with people. He considered that standing up to humans once in a while did some good! Of course, none of the other ponies agreed with him and even Don did not want to take the whole thing too far.

Next morning, after breakfast Susan led all the ponies outside and with other members of staff, escorted them over to some buildings on the other side of the Sanctuary. On the way over, they passed the Captain standing with Old Portly and another little man who was trying to look efficient.

It would appear that on the day, the girls would have the ponies hidden around the corner of a building and when the band started to play their music, they would file out. They were to make their way over to a larger building where there would be crowds of people to cheer them. The Captain would make a speech and then he would walk over and pat each pony on the head. After more speeches, the ponies would be led back towards the stables again. At the stables would be a lady who would cut some tape and declare the stables open. The ponies would then be placed in their stalls.

As much as Don hated all this fuss, he decided that he would not misbehave until the real thing tomorrow. Cocky Bantam was nowhere to be seen so the run through went very well. From the smile on the Captain's face, it was clear he was very pleased with how the plans had worked. They only had to do the rehearsal twice and as there were no hitches, the Captain told Old Portly that he was satisfied the girls knew what to do.

The ponies were led off to the paddocks. Don was beside himself with anger, after having to "do this", "do that", "do the other". Besides, the girl who led him was "horrible." Not once did she let him stop for a mouthful of grass - AND she was constantly digging him to "hurry up!" He was smaller than the other ponies so he was slower. Why should he have to trot in order to catch up and if tomorrow she started, he declared that he would get his own back in some way or other! The other three ponies thought that it went very well.

The cows had seen some of the event and of course they were quite interested in the whole affair. They asked Bluff what it was in aid of and of course Don interrupted and told them to "clear off" and "mind your own business" and this upset them somewhat. But Bluff, being a kind fellow, stopped and explained it to them although at the end of it, they still did not know what it was all about. Don remarked that Bluff had wasted his breath and time on such ignorant creatures. The cows were all for giving Don "a working over" but Bluff and the greys talked them out of it.

That evening when Cocky fluttered up to Bluff's doorway, it was Don who enquired:

"When is it all happening then?"

"It was no good being seen during the pretend-time today" chirped Cocky "because that Susan girl would have locked me up for sure and that was the last thing I wanted her to do. So I kept down in the shrubbery with the others. I did have a good laugh at you lot though, parading up and down like that. The way that girl made Don trot was worth seeing!"

"What are you going to do tomorrow?" asked Don all eager

to know Cocky's plans.

"I'm not in a position to tell you" returned Cocky "in case it gets back to 'you know who'!"

"Who's going to tell her anything?" enquired Don.

"The same rogue who tried to get her to look up in the rafters a few weeks back" snapped Cocky, looking fairly and squarely at Bluff who continued to eat his hay, pretending Cocky was not there.

"Bluff wouldn't do a thing like that" said Don a little indignantly.

"Oh yes I would!" remarked Bluff and the greys snorted their approval.

"There you see" quipped the bantam "that's why I don't tell you lot anything. You'll have to wait until the morning!"

With that he flew up into the rafters so as not to be caught by Susan when she came round to clear the buckets.

"I can't wait for tomorrow" said Don excitedly "To see the Captain's face when he has a revolt on his hand will be quite something!"

"I wouldn't be too sure" remarked Bluff who had been listening quite contentedly. "You see, it will only be a small revolt because there is not much that the wretched bird in the rafters can do.." and this brought an instant reaction from Cocky.

"Who do you think you are calling a wretched bird?" he squawked "and don't be too sure about how much I can do. I have vowed to get equal with that wicked girl and tomorrow I will make her blush to her roots, mainly because Old Portly ordered her to get all the other small animals in for the morning and I will be out!"

"I think you are an evil, good for nothing, scraggy old bird!" snorted Bluff, feeling very cross at the way this feathered fiend was intending to have a go at Susan. Susan of all people was one of the kindest and nicest Bluff had met.

Don enjoyed listening to the bantam's plans and his flanks twitched with excitement. The greys felt like Bluff and were very angry with Cocky. They both decided that if he did hurt poor Susan, they would not let him stay in the stables again.

After Susan had gone home for the night, Bluff and the greys warned Cocky and Don about upsetting anyone the next day but all they heard in reply was giggling and snorting. Those two really had got something arranged for the Captain tomorrow and poor Bluff was so worried.

Chapter 11

What a Welcome!

Cocky had already left when the ponies awoke the next day and they knew that he planned to make himself scarce when the staff came on duty.

Bluff ambled over to the door to see what the weather was like and found that outside there was a very severe frost but it seemed from the way the sun was peeping through the trees in the background, that it was going to be a bright day. Bluff turned his head to the left and saw Bobby looking out from his stall. "Good morning Bob" he greeted.

"Morning Bluff" was the reply. "It's flipping cold out there!"

"You can say that again!" said Bluff, edging back into the stall a little. "Cocky must have left early this morning."

"You know why, don't you?" went on Bobby "he did not want to be seen before the welcoming started."

"Well, all I hope is that he does not overdo his attempts to ruin the Captain's day!" returned Bluff.

"I hope he does!" said a sleepy voice from the next stall and they knew that Don was awake and ready to do his worst.

The sun rose higher but the warmth from it was very weak and the ponies kept well back in their stalls so as not to get cold whilst waiting for their breakfast. Usually when the ground was frosty they were kept inside until the frost had disappeared from the grass, but today it did not matter because they would not go out to graze until the business of being welcomed was over.

The sound of the machines arriving brought them all to the doors so that they could give a neigh to the girls, all, that is except Don. He did not bother, mainly because he could not see over his door at all. To him it was a waste of time doing anything except wait. When it came, the hot bran was most welcome and the greys, who were still getting their beet pulp, felt a lot better for the warmth inside them. Don moaned because he had not even finished his hay net when he was dragged out to be groomed and smartened up! He refused to hold his hooves up and when he did, he put all his weight on them so the girl could not hold them. He tried to bite her backside and in the end, Susan arranged for two girls to see to him, one to hold his head and one to do the work.

The other ponies took it all in good part and Bluff rather enjoyed the fuss of being groomed and cleaned. The greys also appreciated being looked after and they told Don that he was a spoil-sport for not allowing the girls to attend to him. But the little black pony, with a wicked glint in his eye, took great pleasure in teasing them. It was at that moment one of the girls felt a little annoyed with Don and gave him a dig in the ribs which caused the pony to jump and cry out.

"You vicious thing" he yelled and this caused merriment with the other ponies! "Did you lot see what that smelly, strange looking girl did to me?" asked Don. "She poked me very hard for no reason!" he went on, with a hurt feeling in his voice.

"You asked for that Don" smiled Bluff "you've been trying their patience all the morning and when they have a go at you, you don't like it!"

"That's right" put in Bobby "they should have given you a dig a long time ago."

"There is no doubt about it" Don continued "none of these girls who work here has a sense of humour. The whole lot have a very nasty attitude."

All the girls were keyed up and it showed in their haste to get everything cleaned and the ponies made to look the part. There was so much to do and they thought they would never be ready in time.

Susan had counted all the miscellaneous animals and put them in their pens for the morning but she was one short and that was the little bantam cockerel who hung around the stables. She knew that she would have to find him, otherwise the Manager would be angry but find him she could not, even though she had scoured the place. She hoped that he would not be missed and maybe had strayed off somewhere.

The paintwork was washed and the stable area looked a picture. The stalls were spotless and each had a full hay net hanging on the wall and a bucket of pony nuts beside the water trough. The ponies were walked by the girls so that they did not get dirty and each one was wearing a brand new halter with a different coloured lead rope.

The band arrived, dressed in their brightly embroidered uniforms and then the Captain came up and patted each of the ponies on the head. As usual, he looked at their teeth, which upset them because of the aftershave he had on his hands. It caused them all to splutter and spit - much to the annoyance of the girls who were wearing brand new uniforms. Mr. Harry, complete with monocle, arrived which took the heat out of the situation a little because the ponies enjoyed seeing the glass fall from his eye. Mr. Parkin, the farrier, gave them a pat, as though they had just met, causing Don to comment that they were all a bit barmy trying to convince people that they had just arrived.

Old Portly trailed around behind the Captain who was busy shaking hands with all and sundry! Some very large lorries arrived and when the men started unloading their strange looking machines, the ponies remembered that they had seen them the day they left the mines. They were called 'television...' something or other. A man arrived with bits and pieces of wire attached to something called a microphone which made his voice very loud when he talked to it. None of the ponies was at all happy with the noise. The cows in the fields started kicking up a row which Don thought was reasonable, seeing as how the man made so much commotion with his machine. The cows had to be quietened and someone went down to the field to shoo them away. Bluff knew it would take a lot more than a few 'shoo's' to move those old ladies in the field as they had told him previously that they too would join in the event. And join in they did!

None of the ponies had seen so many people.

"There are definitely more here than when we left the mines" said Bluff and he asked the others if they felt cold waiting around. They all replied they did and he told them to start pawing the ground with their feet. They started to do that and, like a miracle, the girls took them around for a walk again.

"I think that Susan looks more nervous than we do" said Bobby.

"Huh, I wouldn't welcome her anywhere! Serves her right! Silly twiddle" snorted Don. Bluff grew annoyed. He thought that she had worked very hard with them in the time they had been together.

"Oh yes" went on Don, becoming equally irritated, "it's all right for you to defend her when she has made you three her pets but what about the way she has treated me and that poor

Bantam then? I've never heard any of you defend us against her!" Don was shaking with anger at his old friend. The girl holding him became worried at his snorting, not knowing of course, that the little pony was in fact talking to his friends. She thought he was going to have a fit and called to Susan. "Oh, don't worry" said Susan "he is most probably laying down the law to his friends." Little did she realise that she had hit the nail right on the head, causing Don to remark -

"Did you lot hear her? That girl can understand us!"

"You had better be careful then, hadn't you!" warned Bluff "or she'll hear all the names you call her!"

The noise in the Sanctuary became louder and louder as the band practised and the man with the microphone started shouting ONE, TWO, THREE, TESTING - TESTING!

"What's he on about?" enquired Bruce.

"How should we know?" answered Bluff "it's all too much for me. I think I'll just stand here and pretend that it is not happening."

"So will I" volunteered Bobby.

The girls were told to take up their positions and quickly walked the ponies across the lawns to wait in line behind the rather large building.

"When you hear me say 'Welcome to South Bunford' I want you to lead the horses out as though you had just arrived" said an unknown voice, with an unfamiliar accent.

"Horses" thought Bluff "the man's an idiot!"

"We haven't just arrived! argued Don.

"We know that" retorted Bruce "but it's their game so we will just have to play along with them!"

"I'm not going to, so there!" snapped Don.

"Ladies and Gentlemen" said the strange voice again. "Today, history will be made in this Sanctuary, when we will welcome to South Bunford four old but very distinguished ponies who have spent many years working for us under the ground, hauling coal trucks so that we can keep warm and so that British industry can keep on producing the goods that mean so much to us......" His voice went on and on.

"What a load of drivel!" thought Don and he was jolted back to reality when the voice said "Welcome to South Bunford our four friends..." and the girls started to walk out. Bluff first, then Bruce, followed by Bobby and then Don. But at that precise moment Don stuck his heels in and would not move. The poor girl tugged at the lead rope and pulled, but no use. The black pony had decided that enough was enough and he just stood there.

"Oh, please come on" begged the girl.

"Clear off you stupid creature" Don snorted and confusion reigned throughout the Sanctuary!

The Captain and Susan dashed forward to urge the pony to go forward and this gave Don the chance he had been waiting for. In an unguarded moment, the Captain's hand went close to Don's muzzle and in a flash, Don grabbed it and held it in a firm grip. The howl of anguish from the Captain was echoed throughout the area. With the injured hand tucked under his armpit, he did a tribal dance round and round, much to the delight of the rebellious pony. Susan grasped Don's lead rope and with a toss of his head, he sent her sprawling on her bottom!

Pandemonium broke out everywhere! What with the Captain still rubbing his fingers, calling for a plaster and Susan who had picked herself up, advancing on the flinching Don with a menacing look in her eye, the producer watching near the television cameras could not get a word in and shouted "CUT, CUT!" Susan was really furious with Don and

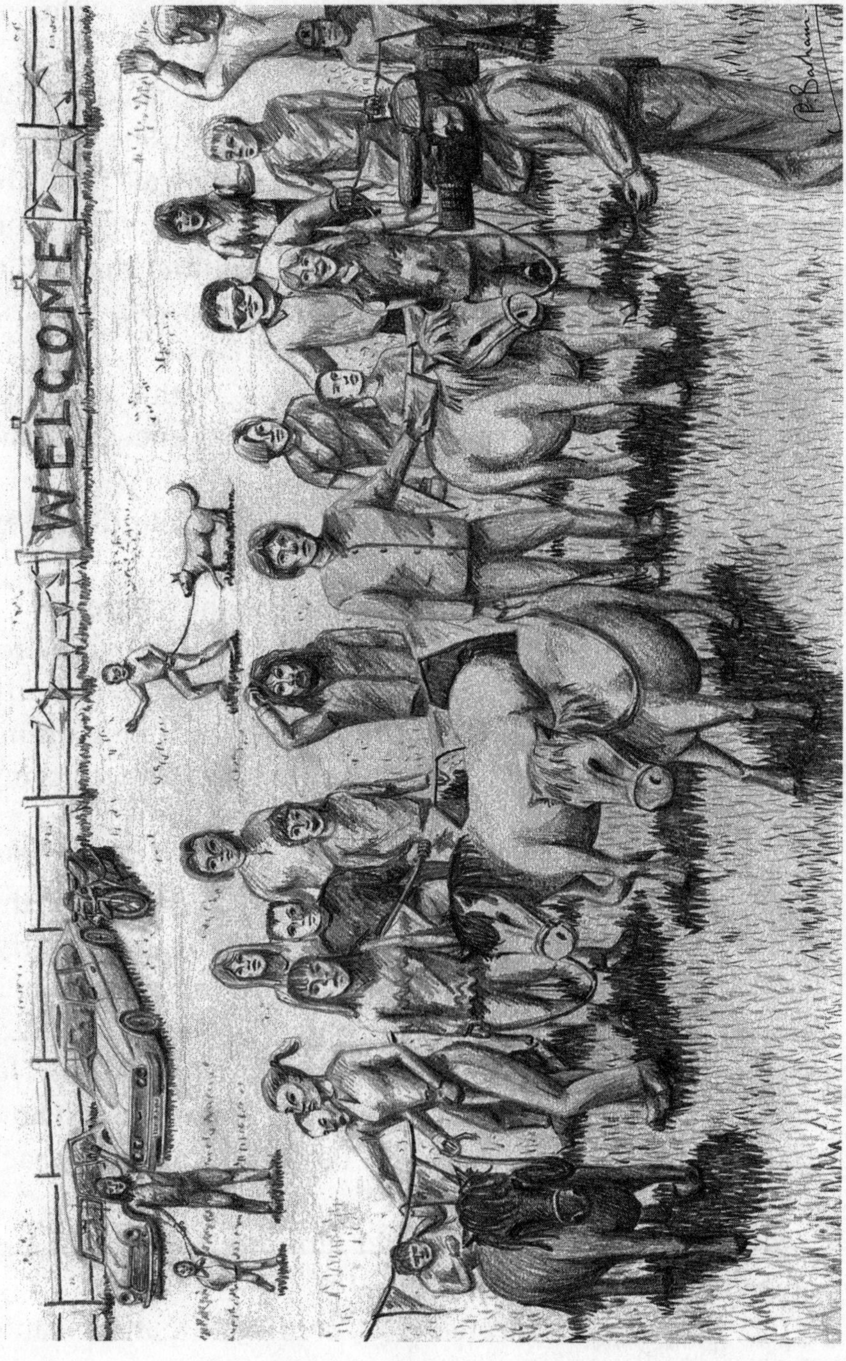
WELCOME

if looks could have killed, then Don would have withered away.

"Get that rotten little pony out of sight!" shouted the producer and Susan led him around the corner. She wagged her finger at Don and said "Don't you dare play me up again you little runt or I'll thrash the daylights out of you!" Don sniggered at that because he knew full well that she would not touch him and was confident that he had won the first round on his own.

"Now, ladies and gentlemen, we must get this 'arriving' done properly" said the producer. The ponies knew that this man was getting annoyed by the tone of his speech.

"Don't you dare play up again Don" called Bluff as they prepared to be led around the building.

"Just watch me!" warned Don and then they were off.

"We welcome to South Bunford our four friends!" repeated the voice on the microphone and away went Bluff, Bruce and Bobby and bringing up the rear, walking on his hind legs was Don, with the poor girl, almost in tears, trying to coax him to walk properly.

"Why isn't that stupid pony walking normally?" shouted the producer. "CUT, CUT. Now look here" he went on to the poor unfortunate girl "you must get him to walk properly. The viewers do not want to see a horse from a rodeo on their screens. They want a poor old pony who has just retired, walking sedately along! Do you understand?" he asked. The poor girl nodded her head but in fact she had no idea of how she was going to cope. Susan gave Bluff to her and came back to lead Don herself.

"You, my little friend" she told him "are a disgrace. Not only to me but to the whole place!"

"Oh, drop dead!" snorted Don, confident that she could

not understand him. He was tickled pink by the way he was holding up the proceedings and preventing these stupid humans from enjoying themselves. The looks he was getting from the other ponies were terrible.

They were taken back behind the building and a man with a funny board in his hand shouted "Ponies Welcome Part One -Take Three" and once again the voice called out the welcome to the ponies and dutifully off went Bluff followed by the two greys and bringing up the rear - or at least he was supposed to be bringing up the rear, was Don who, with a swift trot started to overtake the other ponies causing them to jump sideways. Poor Susan was trying her hardest to hold him back and was beside herself with embarrassment.

"Whoa" she kept shouting but Don had decided to head for the stables and it took Susan, the Captain (still nursing his bitten hand) and Old Portly to stop him!

"You rotten creep" Susan shouted in his ear and the Captain's face was a picture. It was turning a kind of blue with rage and he was really telling Old Portly what he thought of Susan and her handling of Don. Again it was "CUT, CUT" and the faces of those trying to get things organised were a fantastic picture. The television crew thought it very funny but not the producer. HE thought it was a complete waste of his time! "You really must try to control that black horse" he raged.

The Captain was even more furious. He roared: "What do you mean? Do you think we enjoy this pony running amok?"

"It would seem that way" retorted the man, walking away mumbling to himself.

As soon as they arrived at the back of the building again, Susan grabbed Don's halter and shouted as loud as she could. "You horrible little monster! Why are you doing this to me?"

"Good Ho" snorted Don, with great pleasure "I've got this girl really rattled this time!"

Susan had lost her usual composure and her pale colour turned to a deep red as she became more frustrated with the obstinate little creature by the minute.

"Pack it up now" said Bruce turning to Don "you've caused enough upset."

"Not flipping likely" Don merely snorted back "I'm only just starting to enjoy myself."

"Come off it!" warned Bluff, who was starting to feel rather tired with the hanging about, "your stupidity is gradually getting us all down."

"Ponies Welcome, part one, take four" and again the procession started off. This time Don followed as though butter would not melt in his mouth. Smiles appeared all round as they made their way towards the Reception area. Even the Producer was smiling and the people relaxed. All was well.

Arriving at the Reception, the ponies were led round the assembled celebrities who all in turn smiled at them as though they were royalty. Everything was going to plan until Don decided to turn his bottom slightly towards the crowd and then very gently lash out with his hind feet. There were screams, shouts and a general air of panic from the ladies as he somehow managed to balance on his front feet and continue kicking with his hind. He never caught anybody, because he made sure that he did not, but with the hullabaloo, it made the other ponies jump about because they had no idea of what was happening behind them. The man from the television went 'raving mad', especially when one of his camera men was caught up in the melee. "CUT" he screamed "CUT" and the cameras stopped whirring. Our hero had

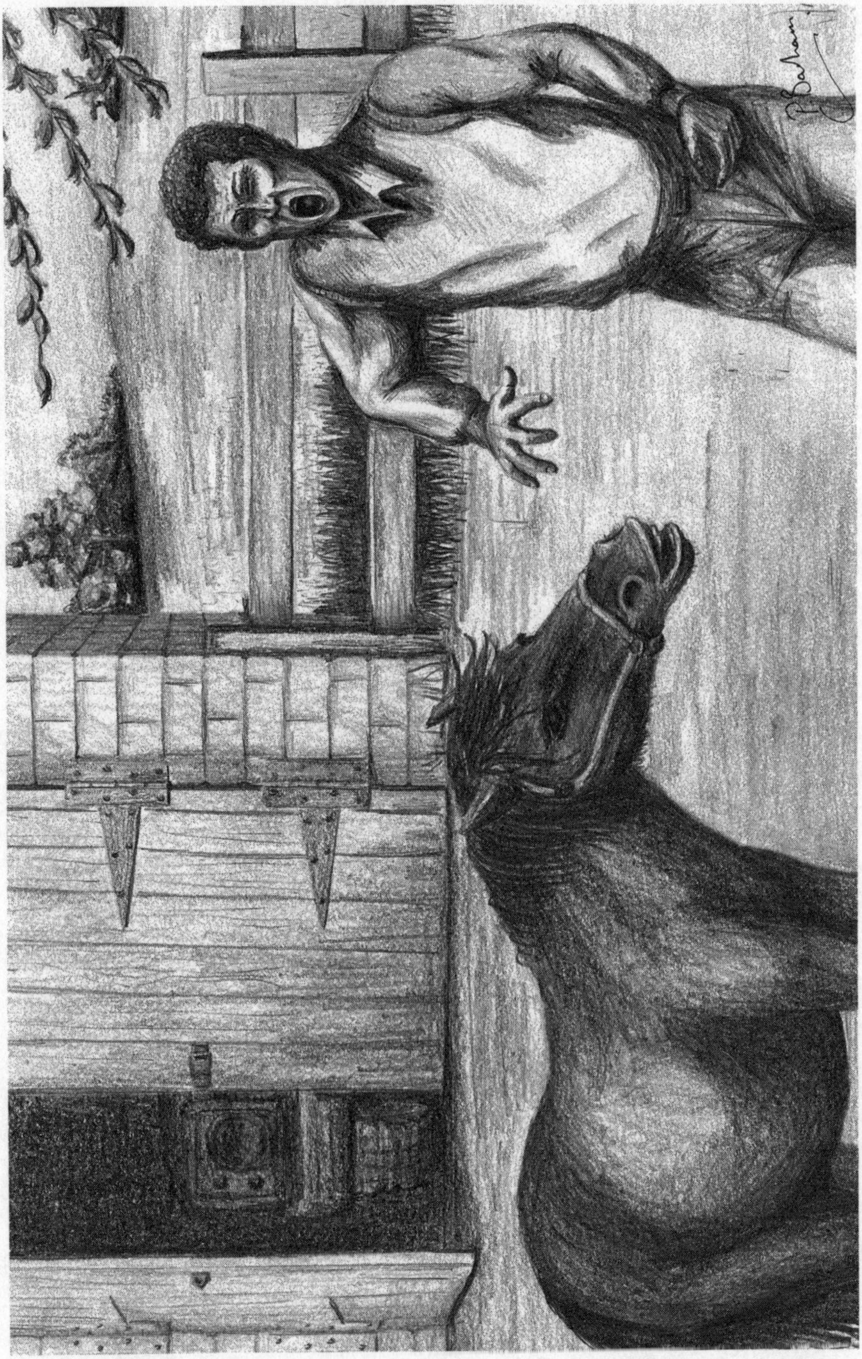

done it again! Susan did not know where to look. Had she caught the Captain's eye she would undoubtedly have dropped through the floor. Old Portly had made a sudden departure and the staff of the Sanctuary were trying to live down the disasters of the last hour.

A Contribution from Cocky...

"If that rotten little pony does one more thing wrong" shouted the Producer "I shall have him put back in his stable!"

"Why not back in the mines!" shouted someone in the crowd.

Meanwhile the bandsmen were also getting tired with playing the same stirring march. Just as they started to play, they had to stop because of the antics of the small black pony. One of the bandsmen remarked that he thought Don was a "Communist" seeing as how he upset everybody so well.

"We will take it from where the horses arrive at the Reception area!" cried the exasperated Producer.

"Welcome to the ponies part one, take five " echoed the man slamming the clapper boards together. Round the ponies went, all sedately and then they were lined up facing a row of microphones. The Captain walked up to the dais and one could see he was trying to compose himself.

"Good morning ladies and gentlemen" he started and just above his head was a very loud "Cock-a-doodle-do" and into view strutted Cocky Bantam, looking resplendent in his neatly preened plumage.

"Good morning ladies and gentlemen" repeated the Captain and again he was interrupted by the ravings of the bantam which, to the people in the crowd, sounded like he was crowing.

To the animals however who could understand him, Cocky was being as rude as he could be to the assembled people. The

Captain started his speech and Cocky in turn started his address to the animals: "Isn't this old geezer a right stuffed shirt!" he called out. "And look at all the others. They are only here for the beer!" he cried. Even the cows down in the field straining to hear what was going on, enjoyed that pun and mooed loudly.

"Can somebody get that chicken off the roof" squealed the Producer. "It is ruining the sound levels and the recording engineer is having dreadful trouble in getting a good track."

One of the staff rushed off at the double to get a ladder and in the meantime the proceedings were held up.

"I enjoyed your caper" Cocky Bantam called out to Don who felt rather pleased that somebody had appreciated his efforts. "I thought you were rather brave and boy, it was fun when you tipped that girl on to her fat bottom!" he giggled. "That was revenge for the times she prodded me out of the rafters." He went on "Are you going to have another go at them?"

"No, he is not!" retorted Bluff very crossly "and we would be grateful if you would take to your wings and clear out of here."

"Hark who's talking!" rebuked Cocky. "Why, it is ugly!"

Just then, the ladder arrived and one of the staff climbed up to dislodge the reluctant bird. No matter how he tried, the hapless man could not catch the bantam and it ended up with the television crew men throwing clods of earth at the luckless bird who, eventually, amid great squawking and shouting, flew off the building over towards the stable block, followed by a couple of staff who had been given orders to apprehend him.

Silence again reigned and the clapper-board man said "Welcome to the ponies, part one take ten." Amid the intervening chaos the Producer had tried to start five other times but no one had really noticed! The Captain's speech went quite well, interrupted only by the cows in the fields who tried hard to stop the event but found themselves chased off. Six people made speeches and none of them said very much of importance, except how marvellous the ponies looked and how young they all seemed. To the ponies it was all a bit of a bore and they wanted it to finish so that they could carry on with their usual day's routine. The band played more loud music and from time to time, the people clapped and it was all rather pleasant.

The Producer said he was pleased with the event so far, apart from "you know who" and wanted to go on to the next part where the ponies were put into the stall by that well known gentleman from the Miners Union, Mr Joe Gormley. It was strange because it was that man's voice the ponies understood so well; all the other speakers spoke as though they had plums in their mouths!

Susan still had not forgiven Don and was dreading what the wretched black pony would do next.

"Let us line up from the Reception area to the stables" said the Producer "and we will do a run through with the horses going to 'their new homes.'" Being called 'horses' angered the ponies to such an extent they felt like doing what Don had already carried out that morning.

"Excuse me" said the Captain "these little fellows are not horses they are ponies and small ones at that."

"So, they are ponies" retorted the Producer sarcastically "what's the difference? They look like small horses to me!"

"It would be nice to refer to them in the correct manner" said a very important looking man, obviously connected to the television people. The ponies found him to be much nicer than the Producer who kept shouting at them and calling them by the wrong names.

"Alright then" continued the Producer with a further hint of sarcasm in his tone "we will do a run through with the ponies going to their new home and I hope that will satisfy our Director who seems to think that what one calls the animals is more important than getting the film in the can!"

The Director was not impressed by that remark. "As soon as the cameras are set up, we will have a dry run so that we can judge the angles accurately. By the way Sound, could you give me the levels and find the best place for the static mikes outside the stables."

The Sound Engineer nodded and started to carry out what had been requested. The Captain and some of the guests were shepherded down the road towards the stables and children from the local school were to line the route and to make it look very busy and crowded.

On the rehearsal, things were not too bad. The Producer shouted at the girls a few times to keep the ponies in line but it all worked reasonably well.

The band moved position and then settled down and the air was alive with their rendition of a famous march which the ponies did not care for too much. "Ponies welcome, Part two, take one" shouted the man with the clapper board. "And action" cried the Producer and the girls started to walk from the Reception down towards the stable area, pretending they had just arrived. Going between rows of children all of whom were trying to grab handfuls of pony, was rather off-putting and it gave Don another excellent opportunity to upset the proceedings. He was passing a little boy with an outsize bag hung round his shoulders and as the boy leaned forward to try and touch the black pony, he struck with the speed of lightning and his teeth found the strap of the bag! Of course, he continued walking, even though Susan was desperately trying to get the bag off him. The little lad found himself being pulled along by this rather obstinate pony!

"Let me go, you 'orrible thing" he shrieked and great confusion was created by Don, who simply refused to allow the strap to slip from his teeth. Susan eventually pulled the bag away and the little boy, obviously shaken, was trying to brush his muddy clothes.

"Wot'll me Mam say?" he sobbed "she didn't want me to come to this stupid place in the beginning."

He tried to recover his composure. One of the lady teachers came forward to console him and above the chatter of a lot of excited young voices, the Producer was shouting to his television crew to start the thing all over again. Susan was beside herself. It just was not her day and she rather felt like crying but was determined not to let the half-pint black pony see her do that. She stifled her tears and wheeled him round to follow the other ponies back to the start again.

"I think we will try the real thing" called the Producer, "so everyone take up their positions and let's try and get the one take." There was a lot of shuffling around and the man with the boards shouted "Welcome to the ponies, Part two, Take two." The Producer then called "And Action..." Away went the ponies and this time the public lining the route had been moved back so as not to offer Don, or the others, an obvious target.

The ponies moved beautifully and everyone was pleased. As they arrived at the stables there was a great feeling that at last they had got it right. The Captain ran forward to help the Chairman of the Coal Board and the President of the Mine Workers Union to get to the microphones. Local press men who, up till then, had been kept in the background surged forward to get as many snaps and pictures as they could. The television cameras whirred away and the children were all waving Union Jacks and cheering as loudly as they could. The noise became a crescendo! For the ponies, it was rather frightening and out in the fields the cows were rushing about, bucking and kicking and trying to get in on the festivities.

Bluff consoled Bobby and Bruce who were getting a little restless with all the turmoil and Don was doing his best to grab anything that came within reach. He had some success especially with ladies gloves, coat pockets etc. all of which tasted horrible.

As soon as the Captain went to introduce his special guests, who should appear on the roof of the stables, having evaded all earlier attempts to catch him, none other than Cocky Bantam in all his glory. The Captain put his hands over his eyes and was heard to mutter "Oh, God - not again" and the voice screeched out something like "Can't someone catch that b..... thing!" to which there was a gasp from the assembled crowd. To the human ear, Cocky was making a really nasty noise but to the animals he was shouting as loud as he could, calling all and sundry everything he could lay his tongue to, especially that twit who had tried to catch him up at the Reception and again down here. All the time Cocky's tirade was going on, the other animals enjoyed every moment. The humans were only upset by the noise, not from what Cocky was saying because they could not understand him anyhow. Again, the ladder was brought and the luckless man called Bill was ordered up. "Clear off you bald-headed old coot" screamed Cocky, keeping well out of the way of the tottering Bill, who was not enjoying an enormous round of applause from the crowd. He was rather embarrassed by it all because he was a very shy person. "Come on, Bill!" called the Captain "hurry up and catch the blighter or else it will be dark."

The poor man made every effort in trying to silence the bantam but in his anxious moments, he nearly fell off the ladder head first. Cocky knew he only had a short time in which to make his protests and already he was contemplating his avenue of escape. A glance showed that a quick flight over and towards the hen houses would possibly be his best route. The fellow Bill was nothing, if not a 'tryer,' and he just would not give up so Cocky, with one last scream of "Power to the Ponies!" flew off and a sigh of relief went up from the people. Bill wiped his brow.

The Captain looked towards the Producer whose voice had almost disappeared and waited for his 'say-so' before carrying on with the ceremony. The poor Captain by this time was a nervous wreck. How could it all have gone so badly wrong he asked himself. The Producer was having words with his Director who seemed to enjoy the animal interruptions immensely and told the Producer that it would make good television.

"Not on your life" replied the Producer. "When I have edited this lot, it will seem like a tea party in the vicarage." Then he stormed off thinking how ridiculous it was to work with animals and children. You just could not win.

The ponies felt that it was more like pay day at the pit than a ceremony of welcome and Don declared that he "knew it was going to be useless from the beginning!"

"Who made it useless?" remarked Bluff "only you and that cocky little bantam friend of yours. If it had not been for you two, we would have been finished hours ago and by now in the paddocks having a decent meal of grass. But no, thanks to you two, we are still standing here looking like fools."

The other ponies could tell how furious Bluff was and he never stopped nodding his head all the time he was talking. The two main welcoming speeches to the new stables went off very quietly with both speakers praising the quality of life that was going to be open to the ponies, and thanking the Captain for allowing the Sanctuary to have made them available. Don came in for some "stick" from both of them which brought a snigger from the crowd as well as the ponies. Cocky Bantam was mentioned by the Chairman of the Coal Board who thought that little birds should be seen and not heard! That remark brought a fair amount of applause from the assembled crowd. As soon as the ribbon leading to the stalls was cut, all four ponies were led into the one with his respective name on it and they had to pretend that it was their first visit. "What a load of old nonsense" thought Don, but he went along with it for the sake of some peace and quiet.

With the ponies safely inside the stable block the staff could be seen to relax and breathe a sigh of relief! All they hoped for now was that no-one would offer their hands to the ponies - especially to Don. The whole crowd relaxed and small groups of people joined together and a string of introductions took place with such comments as "Jolly good show, what" and "It went orf fraightfully well, I thought.." mixed with sentiments like "I'd 'ave cheerfully wrung that flippin' bantam's neck" which brought forth murmurs of "Tut-tut" from those within earshot and "Di'n't that 'orrible little black pony play up!" from the little boy whose bag strap was broken.

The VIP element made their way back to the Reception area where liquid refreshments were available. The children from the local school were formed into pairs and with the

Headmaster at their rear, set off for home. Most of the children were convinced that they would be on the 'tele' that night and the excitement grew minute by minute.

Despite the troubles, even the Producer considered it had been worth it after all. He was sure that after editing the film they had taken, they would be able to put out a really good show on the six-o-clock "Tonight" programme.

The TV men started to dismantle their equipment and the band who had just completed a selection of marches from the First World War, decided to call it a day. All of them were frozen with the cold.

As for the ponies, they had not yet started to discuss what had happened. They stood in their stalls idly munching their hay and keeping well away from the door which was still besieged by people anxious to pat them on the head and pull their ears. The other little animals who, up to this time, had been locked away, were let out to roam around the Sanctuary and of course as soon as they were free, they all crowded around Cocky Bantam, asking him to tell them about his exploits. He loved the limelight and of course he exaggerated everything to twice its size.

The Sanctuary started to get back to normal and the people were drifting away. Mr. Harry the vet and Mr. Parkin the farrier were both presented to the celebrities and afterwards came to the stables to bid their farewells. The Captain came and whilst he spoke very nicely to the other three, Don knew that he was going to have 'words' with him before he left. He did. "You cantankerous little devil" the Captain snarled. "You tried your hardest to stop my ceremony, didn't you?"

Don, although feeling scared inside, thought the best thing to do was to carry on eating and pretend that his tormentor was not there.

"If I had guessed that you would have played us up like that" the Captain raged "I would have left you at the pits!"

Don merely turned his head and gazed at the Captain with contempt. Frustrated with the pony, the Captain marched away muttering under his breath.

As soon as everyone had gone, Susan, with her colleagues, came to put the ponies out to graze. It was Don who became the hero of the field with the cows crowding around, listening to his account of the morning. Bluff and the greys walked away in disgust. How could he be so proud of his behaviour thought Bluff. How could anyone be proud of spoiling what could have been a super day. Bluff felt sorry for Susan who had really taken a lot from that silly little pony during the morning.

"Maybe Susan will go away from the Sanctuary" suggested Bobby.

"Oh, don't say that" Bluff gasped. "Whatever would we do. She has been so good to us."

"Yes, and it's all because of him over there!" declared Bruce. "You know, sometimes he makes me sick!"

The very thought of Susan leaving the Sanctuary brought a deep depression over Bluff for the rest of that day.

When the ponies had been brought in from the paddocks and groomed, Bluff made sure he gave Susan a special nuzzle and for her part she flung her arms around his neck and said "You are a smashing old Bluff, you really are!"

Bluff thought he detected a tear in her eye when she said it. Both the greys made a fuss of her which she seemed to like and Don kept well out of her way when she entered his stall, half expecting to get a "clip round the ear!" Little did he know that Susan never held grudges and in her way, she still loved Don very much but she had to be firm with him otherwise he would let her down all the time and that she would not like.

Cocky fluttered up after Susan had left the stables. "Thought I would leave it a bit late tonight" he cackled "just in case that wretched girl and that Bill fellow decided to have a go at me."

Bluff just could not be bothered to reply. He knew that the sole topic of conversation tonight would be how well those two had done at the ceremony and all the exaggeration and bragging would get on his nerves. The greys felt exactly the same and contented themselves to browsing through their hay net.

When Cocky found that he was not going to have an attentive audience in Bluff and the two greys, he flew across to Don's door and settled down to a good old fashioned chin wag.

"Hey up, old mate!" he said "I thought we scored a notable triumph today."

"We did that" agreed Don, only too pleased to relate the experience all over again to whoever would listen. "I thought your efforts were most praiseworthy, Cocky" he went on, hoping to have a return of compliments from the bantam.

"And yours" replied Cocky "I thought the way you played that girl up was fantastic. I couldn't have done better myself!"

"Thank you" said Don, trying hard not to sound too big-headed. "I did feel that I had got one over on her."

"I should say you did" continued Cocky, piling up the flattery "and you grabbed the Captain and that horrible little boy as well. I laughed so much I thought I would wet myself!"

Don glowed with pride and their boasting conversation went on for a long time before Cocky had to say goodnight and settle down in the rafters. Don felt very pleased with himself and proud in a funny way to think that he had struck a blow for "pony power", whatever that meant.

For many days after the event, both Don and Cocky were treated with great respect by all the other animals who had witnessed or heard about the trouble they had caused. They were always surrounded by admiring fans. Of course Don and Cocky, being who they were, never for one moment shirked their duty in recounting over and over again their exploits of that momentous day.

Chapter 12

Taken for a Ride

Unknown to Don, there were two little girls who lived close by the Sanctuary. They had noticed the ponies in the field and had taken a fancy to them, especially the small black Shetland. They planned to catch him and ride on his back. Although they were only young, about eight or nine years old, they were very devious. Each day they walked down the lane which ran alongside the paddocks and made a note of how close the ponies came to the fence.

The girls went into the Sanctuary and asked lots of questions about the 'poor ponies', trying to learn as much as they could about them.

"Have they ever been ridden?" asked one.

"No" came the answer.

"Are they friendly?" enquired the other.

"Oh yes" said the girl from behind the desk.

"Er, excuse me, do they like titbits?" queried an angelic little voice.

"They do enjoy apples and carrots but visitors are asked not to feed them and certainly not Don who is on a special diet." was the reply.

The two girls chose to ignore the last warning, and having heard what they really wanted to know, they left.

The young member of staff who had met them remarked: "What nice little girls they were and so interested in the ponies too!"

Armed with this most valuable information, the terrible two were hatching a plot to have a ride on Don.

"I bet he wouldn't mind us having a ride" said Lisa.

"I bet he would" remarked Joanne.

"I know what" went on Lisa "let's go and get my sister. She knows all about horses and ponies 'cos she's had lessons!"

"I am not too keen on that" declared a downhearted Joanne. "You know what she's like. She won't let us have a go at all!"

"Of course she will" said Lisa confidently "she isn't that bad!"

"Well, I reckon she is" replied Joanne, definitely not convinced by her friend's assurance.

The two girls sped home and found Lisa's elder sister, Melanie, reading. With great excitement she was let into the secret and sworn to 'secrecy'! Joanne was all for Melanie taking the oath that she and Lisa had already taken. Melanie, at first, refused point blank to take part in what she thought was a silly childish prank. After saying that she would not reveal their devious plan, she was let in on the plot and then agreed to help. She even convinced Joanne that she too should be allowed to have a ride. The only problem was being caught by the Sanctuary staff. So all three decided there and then to devise an escape route should things go wrong.

In the meantime, whilst the three girls took more and more notice of the ponies, Don was quite oblivious to what was being concocted. He even remarked to the others what sweet little people they were; always at the fence that ran by the lane and always smiling and calling over to him. As soon as Don caught a whiff of something to eat being offered, he strolled over, taking his time. He did not want them to think that it was just for the food. He stopped here and there to nibble at the grass whilst his eyes were on the things that the sweet little children were offering. "I must make sure that I do not nip their fingers" he thought, as he gently took a juicy carrot from one and an apple from another. He was just about to savour a second carrot when something landed on his back. Poor Don. He nearly leapt out of his skin and suddenly all four feet left the ground at once. It was not long before he realised that the largest of the three had jumped from the fence, clean on to his back. The carrot was forgotten as he decided to get rid of this burden thrust upon him. Lowering his head, he bucked for all he was worth but the girl had grabbed his mane and was holding tight.

"Get off, you wretched creature!" Don snorted as he jumped for all he was worth.

"Hold on Melanie" the other girls shouted and it became a battle of wits.

Meanwhile the fracas had attracted the other ponies. The cows, who were also watching Don jump around, thought it was a good idea and they started to copy him. The girl remained on Don's back for quite a while before the ache in her hands forced her to let go and slide gracefully to the ground.

Don galloped over to his three friends gasping. "Did you lot see that? What a rotten liberty. You can't trust anybody round here, can you?" There was no answer from the others because they were all giggling so much. None of them thought the old black pony was capable of the gymnastic display he had just given them. They thought the girl deserved their admiration because she had held on for so long.

Don stood with his sides heaving! He was absolutely furious at the girls for daring to get on his back AND to show him up in front of not only his friends, but also the cows who were pulling his leg over his failure to dislodge the girl once she was on his back.

"You rotten, good for nothing, lot of tricksters!" he stormed and decided to trot over the furthest side of the field away from the presence of people. Meanwhile, Bluff had sauntered to where the little people were sitting on the fence, all pleased with themselves. The two smaller ones were looking at the older one with great admiration.

"Gosh, Lisa" said Joanne "your sister is really super. Melanie, how did you manage to hold on for so long?"

"I think it was because I was frightened!" the older girl confessed. "Besides, he is so fat you can't get your legs to grip him. I had to hold his mane tight!"

"You could see he was furious" laughed Joanne, pointing to a fast disappearing Don. "Look at him! I bet he won't come near us again!"

"Oh yes, he will" said a confident Lisa "when he smells food, he will forget today. Just you wait and see!"

With that they saw one of the staff come into the field so they made a quick departure before they were seen.

Susan was very puzzled as to why Don was out of breath when she went to bring him in AND why he was way across the field, away from the others who were all bunched near the fence by the lane. If she could have understood Don, she would have known because he was really having a go about "... her measly kind who waylay poor old ponies and then take advantage of them" but she merely took his snorts to be a part of his high spirits. But why it was only Don out of the four she could not imagine.

When Don told Cocky that night of how these enormous people tried to get on his back he was rather annoyed when Cocky said that he had seen the whole thing and was amazed at the way the bigger of the girls had stayed on so long, despite Don's antics to get her off. Cocky hurt him most by saying: "It shows that you are getting old Don when you cannot unseat a little person like that!"

"Ggetting old?" spluttered Don "I ccould sstill cclobber yyou if yyou ccame cclose enough!"

"Of course you could!" said the bantam "that's because I am so much smaller than you. But you know very well that you could never catch me so you are able to boast like that!

"Oh, go to sleep!" retorted an irritated Don.

The next day, despite all his shouting to the contrary, Don was almost fooled when the three girls appeared with more lovely smelling titbits. In fact, he was within about five feet of them, with his mouth already watering, when his mind flew back to the previous afternoon and he stopped dead. "Oh no" he thought " you're not catching me that way" and moved off. To his surprise Bluff calmly walked up to where the three girls were sitting and nibbled at an out-stretched carrot. "You devious nasty thing" blurted out Don as Bluff carefully took an apple from one of the little people. "What are you doing?" he shouted and his eyes nearly popped out of his head as one of the trio crept off the fence and on to the pony's back. "Kick her off" shrieked Don. "Why don't you leap about a bit?" Bluff just stood there accepting more and more of the tasty delicious morsels and seemed quite unconcerned that sitting on his back was a small girl.

After a while, the girls changed places and Bluff even walked around a bit, which caused great excitement among the little people. The more Bluff responded to their plans, the more he was given to eat and what is more, he was thoroughly enjoying the whole thing. Don, standing just out of reach with saliva pouring from his mouth, could stand it no longer. He nudged forward and nothing happened. He nudged forward a little more and just as he was going to get his teeth into a nice juicy apple, one of the other girls pounced and was on his back. Like a shot from a gun, he was away only this time he was galloping and the person on his back was urging him on.

"I'll flipping well get you off!" he said and the luckless pony dug his front hooves in and stopped dead. He felt the weight of the rider leaving him and CRASH, she landed on the grass. To his surprise she jumped up and tried to get on him again. Enough was enough so without any more fuss, Don was away (and the language he used about the girl was dreadful).

Bobby and Bruce both fell for the charms of all three who had no intention of hurting them. They made no attempt to sit on the greys as they had had such a wonderful time with Bluff who seemed to enjoy it as much as they did.

By "going home" time, Bluff and the greys had consumed quite a number of apples, carrots and sugar lumps. Apart from a few bruises on Melanie's bottom, the three friends had spent an enjoyable afternoon with the ponies, except for Don who had taken himself off to sulk on the other side of the paddocks.

"Never mind" said Melanie "we will get him yet" and they went home to tea.

Once again, Susan could not understand why Don was on one side of the paddock and others by the fence next to the lane. Cocky made no mention of the day to Don and he in return decided that he would not converse with the other ponies. He was not pleased at the way they had made friends with the little people, whose sole intentions were to get on their backs and be a nuisance.

Chapter 13

Dial 999 - Emergency

The accident to Bruce made the news in the next few days and cast a shadow over the Sanctuary.

Susan collected the ponies at her usual time and, as was her habit, tied them up outside their stalls so that she could groom and clean them. As Bruce and Bobby had always used the same box owing to Bobby being so nervous, Bruce was tethered outside the barn. It had been a windy day and it was almost gale force by late afternoon. Susan was cleaning Bluff's hooves and so she never saw exactly what happened but she heard an almighty C R A S H followed by an horrendous scream which sent shivers running down her spine. Looking back, for a split second she saw Bruce standing with the overhang, a section of the roof which extended over the front of the barn, laying across him! He fell to the ground and then tried to get up, crying out at the same time. Leaving Bluff, she ran to Bruce. There was blood everywhere. Her immediate reaction was to panic but she told herself to stay calm and cool. The overhang was far too heavy for her to lift and the poor old fellow was well and truly pinned down. Susan shouted as loud as her lungs would allow and continued to shout whilst she tried to think what to do. One of her colleagues appeared and she quickly told her to phone the vet, the Fire Brigade and inform the Manager.

The other poor girl, being comparatively new, did not know which to do first so she ran back to Reception. Within

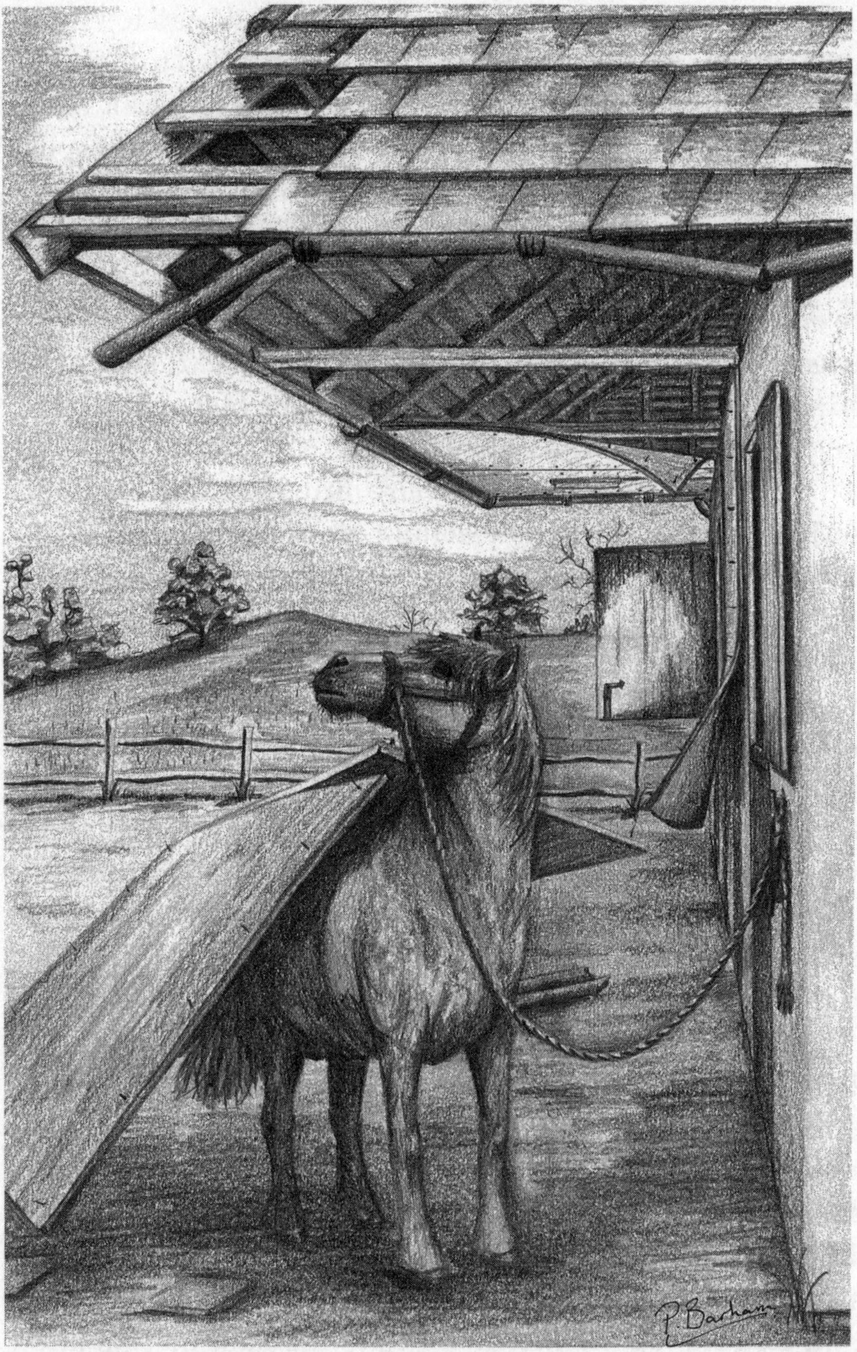
P. Barham

seconds, the staff were on the scene; some started to put the other ponies into their stalls and one was detailed to look after Bobby, who had already started to become hysterical. Susan knelt by Bruce and took his head into her arms and spoke softly into his ear. The poor grey pony was virtually exhausted by his efforts to get off the ground. Although the staff tried to lift the overhang, it was no use. All they could do was to ease some of the strain. Susan knew that the longer Bruce was trapped, the more the likelihood of his heart giving out, so she directed all her energies to pacifying him and trying to give him courage whilst they waited.

The telltale sounds of the Fire Brigade came as a very welcome relief to her now aching arms and she hoped that the vet would soon be there as well. The ponies in the stables sensed that something serious had happened and they all stood at the back of their stalls and hung their heads, as if they were all praying for their old friend trapped nearby. Somehow the three ponies drew a lot of comfort from hearing human voices and all their own feelings seemed to leave them and they concentrated on the humans outside, hoping they would do something. Not even the noise of the Fire Brigade with their sirens wailing brought the three ponies out of their solitude; it was as if they were willing Bruce to hold on and fight as hard as he could.

The Firemen were soon rigging up a block and tackle to hoist the hangover and Bruce had started to cry out again.

A screech of car brakes heralded the vet who, this time was not Mr. Harry, but Mr. David his Australian partner, whose knowledge of ponies was immense. He quickly came over to Bruce and with his unusual quiet Australian accent, started to talk to the old pony. He gave Bruce a shot to help his heart and a strong pain killer to alleviate the pain that he knew would follow. "Steady up Blue" he called softly "we'll soon get you out of this bother." His voice, merging with the closeness of Susan, seemed to give the pony vital reassurance.

"Tell us when you want us to start lifting Mr. David" the Chief Fire Officer called. Mr. David turned and with a motion from his hand, signalled for the strain to be taken and slowly the heavy weight started to rise. "As soon as the old fellow feels the weight going" he told Susan" he will want to try and get up, and that is what we don't want at this stage." Susan understood and still with her arms around the pony's neck she restrained him. "I want hot water by the bucket, swabs and sterile towelling" called Mr. David to the staff who were watching nearby "and as quick as you can!" The staff scurried away to do his bidding.

There was no doubt about it, Bruce had been badly cut and grazed by the falling overhang and Mr. David was afraid that the pony's leg may have been broken which would most probably have meant that Bruce would have to be put to sleep. As soon as he voiced that opinion, Susan, whose composure up until that time had been ice cool, broke down and tears welled up in her eyes.

"Please don't let anything happen like that Mr. David, please" she wept. The pleading in her voice touched him very deeply.

"Come on girl, that is no way to be. This pony needs you to be strong, not crying all over him" he said. With a sob Susan tried to pull herself together, and choking back her tears she tried not to permit her voice to falter as she spoke quietly to the old warrior. Buckets began arriving also towels and Mr. David began exploring the damage. He decided that because of the pony's apprehension, he would have to give him an injection that would put him into a long sleep whilst he carried out his work. Bruce seemed to sigh with relief as the drug took effect and Susan was able to relax her vigil and help Mr. David.

The cuts were quite extensive and all the staff held their breath as the vet examined the old pony to see if he had a break in his leg. Susan had her fingers crossed so tight that her knuckles turned white. With utmost care, Mr. David looked all over the leg and hind quarters and a great sigh of relief went up when at last he pronounced "Well, there are no breaks as far as I can ascertain but we've got a lot of stitching to do" and he started preparing his sutures. Willing hands helped as each cut and graze was cleaned. It took over an hour to dress and suture all the wounds. Straw was placed around the pony and his head was supported. Slowly he came round. The vet said that once Bruce was standing up, he would have a better idea about the leg. Mr. Harry joined Mr. David and both vets had a discussion. Susan could not hear what was said but there was a lot of head nodding and it appeared that Mr. Harry agreed with what Mr. David had done.

It seemed an eternity before Bruce attempted to rise but when he did it took him quite a time because he was so tottery on his feet. He had not broken anything, however, and was gently eased into his stall. The other ponies had sensed that all was well.

The Fire Brigade had been splendid and had moved the offending overhang well out of the way and the builders had been told of the accident. Having done all he could for the time being, Mr. David said he would call in later during the evening to give Bruce some more pain killing injections and to check him over. Mr. Harry remarked what a strong old character he was and for the first time in many hours, smiles could be seen on the faces of the Sanctuary staff but not on

Susan's - she was too busy fussing around him.

As for Bruce, he could not remember anything of the accident and the first thing he could recall was Susan with her arms around his neck whispering to him. He did faintly remember though a feeling that he would never get out of the affair without something terrible happening and he had felt like panicking, partly out of the feeling of being trapped. He had a horse-sized headache and felt he just wanted to stand and be quiet. His leg and backside hurt a lot and he felt very sore, as though he had been kicked by one of the others.

"Do you know what happened to you?" asked Bobby.

"Not really" replied Bruce.

"Well, the ceiling thing fell on top of you" returned Bobby, his voice getting rather excited. "And the people had a job to get it off you" he went on. Bruce was no wiser because he just had no idea of what happened and with the drugs still in his bloodstream, even Bobby's voice was becoming muzzy. Mr. David returned later in the evening and gave Bruce another pain killer and listened to his heart and made sure that he would be alright. He told Susan that complete rest was what the pony needed for the time being but he would come in again first thing in the morning. Susan asked if she should stay but the vet thought it would be much better if she were to leave him. "Anyhow" said Mr. David "the Manager always walks round and if anything is wrong, he can always call me" and with that Susan felt better. She would not mind going home because after all the emotional upset, she was very tired and hungry. She realised that she had eaten nothing since the whole dreadful episode had happened.

For several days, Bruce was kept in his stall and unlike him, he made no fuss when he saw the other three ponies going out to the paddocks in the morning. It was as if he knew that being kept in was doing him good. Mr. David asked Susan to lead him slowly round the stable area after five days and was extremely pleased with his progress. Each day Bruce felt stronger and on the tenth day, Mr. David removed all the stitches and apart from the bald patches where his coat had been shaved off, he felt pretty good - not well enough to gallop yet - but very much better. His confidence was coming back and the only fear he really had was of standing under the overhang but as the builders had been back and secured it, that fear was slowly disappearing.

Bruce was kept up to date with all the news from his old friends and from Cocky Bantam who had taken to talking to him more than he did to Bluff these days. Cocky considered that poor Bruce was feeling out of things.

It would appear that the three little people had continued their devious tricks to ride on Bluff's back and each day they offered numerous titbits in order to attract the old pony over to them. Bluff enjoyed it but Don was absolutely livid. He stood back and snorted many rude things to the three girls and it was a good thing they could not understand him. Most of the remarks he muttered were because he could not get his fair share of the treats they had to give and every time he dared to get near, they tried to ride on his back. Don totally objected to that. Bobby received his share of the carrots and apples because he allowed the bigger of the three a ride on him.

The whole escapade went on for some time until one day Susan, who had spent so much of her day nursing Bruce, decided she would visit the three lads in the paddock. As she arrived, she looked across the field by the lane and saw one girl on Bluff's back and the larger one on Bobby's. She nearly burst a blood vessel!

"Hey," she shouted "what on earth are you doing?" As soon as the terrible trio heard her shout, they put operation escape into effect and rushed off.

"Come back here" cried the breathless Susan, shouting at the fleeing figures but no way were those intrepid girls going to stop. Susan stood and panted. She then understood why Don was often to be found across the paddocks when she brought the ponies in; it was because he did not like people riding on his back and that was exactly what had been happening. No wonder Bluff and Bobby belched every night they came back - they were full of carrots, apples and other titbits offered as a bribe for a ride.   Susan initially was very angry but considered that as she had now discovered what had been happening and no harm had been done, she would be more vigilant in future. She decided not to tell the Manager but would just keep an eye open for the girls and warn them if they did it again. The only pony who was pleased with the three getting found out was Don, who even complained that "it had taken the stupid girl long enough to catch on to what was going on!" Bluff and Bobby felt sorry that they would lose their tasty 'extras' and both of them commented that they could hardly feel the girls on their backs anyway so they could not understand why Don was so sensitive about it. Don replied that it was the principle of the thing that mattered!

"Do you mean that you are now putting principles before your stomach?" asked Bluff.

"I think that question is somewhat rude and I decline to answer" retorted Don. This brought a guffaw from the others and from the roof came the remark "The truth always hurts!"

"Shut up, Cocky. You are just a trouble-maker" said Don to which the cackling told its own story.

"Do you realise Don, that you are your own worst enemy and that you are more fickle than a filly!" continued Bluff. "You seem to change the rules just to suit yourself!"

"Why don't you just belt up Bluff" was Don's curt reply.

"Why should I?" queried Bluff "I'm only telling you the truth."

"Well I am not partial to you telling me the truth!" returned Don, all confused. He was quite convinced that all of them were against him. Bruce was now taking more interest in the conversations and he had his own news to tell them.

"What is it old son?" enquired Bluff.

"Well" went on Bruce, feeling very happy "I'm going to join you in the paddocks tomorrow."

"Whoopee" shouted Bobby.

"Jolly good show" said Bluff.

"Well done!" called Don above the din of a "Cock-a-doodle-do" from the roof. Bruce was pleased and snorted his pleasure.

"You do you realise, my friend Bruce" interjected Cocky "that on that fateful day when half the stables fell on top of you, you were nearly a 'goner', don't you?"

"No" replied Bruce "I didn't realise that."

"Oh yes" went on the bantam "I heard that funny sounding doctor fella telling that girl he thought you might have to go." A cold shiver swept through Bruce as he thought of the possibilities of his demise.

"I must say" broke in Bluff "you put things in a most delicate way, Cocky!"

"Oh, thank you" replied Cocky, feeling pleased that Bluff appreciated his verbal attributes.

"I meant" sneered Bluff "you are like a Shire horse in a china shop!"

"What does that mean?" enquired Cocky puzzled.

"It means that you are stupid" retorted Don.

"How come you think I'm stupid?" asked Cocky.

"Because you are - you silly bird-brained chicken" snapped Don.

"Steady on there" cried Cocky "who do you think you are, calling me a chicken?" It was obvious one could call the bantam anything but NEVER a chicken! Don could not understand why.

"I was not really as bad as Cocky said was I?" asked Bruce.

"No, of course you weren't" said Bobby. "You know Cocky is always the one for creating mountains out of mole hills!"

"Yes, but there must have been something in it for him to say it" went on Bruce, still feeling unmistakenly shaken up with Cocky's statement.

"All you had wrong" interrupted Bluff, trying to take the sting out of the conversation "was cuts, bruises and a few minor grazes. I know that was a fact because I also heard that strange sounding young doctor tell Susan."

Bruce felt reassured and decided he would not listen to anything that Cocky told him again and set about forgetting the whole subject.

It was surprising how the ponies and cows helped Bruce back to normality when he re-entered the paddocks. It was obvious by the way he held his head up and seemed to be savouring the lovely clean air that he had missed his freedom out in the fields. Bobby was his constant companion and, if anything, fussed over him just a little too much. All the other animals kept going up to the old grey, asking him if he was feeling better. In a way, Bruce enjoyed that kind of fuss and although he felt twinges from his injuries, he tried not to dwell on them too much.

Chapter 14

Fox

A few days later, around about going-home time, Cocky failed to appear and the ponies heard from a passing hen that something dreadful had happened to him! Although Bluff and Don in particular liked having 'a go' at the silly bantam, they were eager to know just what had beset the poor little creature.

It appeared from the elderly hen that Cocky had left the main group of bantams and chickens and had gone off to scratch in a pile of dead leaves left by the gardener alongside the Rose Garden. It was whilst he was deeply engrossed in his scratching that a fox which had actually been in the Rose Garden pounced on him and grabbed his tail feathers. Cocky screamed blue murder and leapt about ten feet in the air leaving the fox with a mouthful of his feathers. The fox had immediately chased the poor little bird in a vain attempt to catch him for supper but the timely intervention of the gardener, who had come for his leaves, saved the bantam from a terrible fate. He was left badly shaken up and had a nasty bite mark on his bottom! Cocky had then been taken over to the Animal Hospital and as far as the hen knew, he was still there.

Bluff was very cross because on many afternoons, the ponies had seen that particular fox crossing the paddocks. As all the occupants in the Sanctuary seemed to live happily together, not once did the ponies think the fox would make trouble.

"I will tell you what we are going to do" said Bluff in his very authoritative voice "we are going to teach that fox a lesson which he will not forget in a hurry."

"Hahum. What are we going to do then?" enquired Don, thinking it would be nice to know what Bluff had let him in for.

"WE" went on Bluff, putting a lot of emphasis on the "WE", "are going to kick that wretched fox right out of the paddock every time we see him in there!"

"Oh, yes?" echoed Don, still not too brave about the idea.

"Yes" reiterated Bluff "we are!"

"Does that include we two?" asked Bobby timidly.

"Of course it does" snapped Bluff "we must help poor Cocky! It doesn't matter how many times we disagree with the cantankerous little rascal. It is our duty to protect him and the other animals in the Sanctuary."

Don's mouth had fallen open. He had never heard Bluff put on a "professor-type" voice before and he was really laying the law down.

"Hoorah" said Bobby "well said Bluff, I am with you and so is Bruce, aren't you Bruce?"

"Err, err, well yes, I expect I am" returned the other grey, rather surprised by his brother's instant acceptance of the directive.

"Right then" went on Bluff, rather pleased with himself and with the way he had seized the initiative and had taken over. "This is what I propose we do."

"Firstly, we will split up out in the paddock so that we have a good all round view of where the blighter comes in. Secondly, as soon as one of us sees him, we will alert the others."

"Will we have a kind of secret code?" asked Bobby timidly.

"Don't be so silly" continued Bluff, a little annoyed that his train of thought had been interrupted by such a stupid question. "We will just whinny as loud as we can. As soon as the one seeing the fox has raised the alarm, then that pony will automatically go in kicking until the fox leaves the paddock. But remember, let it know why we are taking this action." Bluff was trying to think whether or not he had covered every point.

"Sounds great to me" said Don, feeling a little better now that Bluff had explained his plan. After all, Don always did like a good kick even if he did only have short legs.

Bruce did mention the fact that he did not expect he would be able to take too active a part in the operation because of his incapacity. The other three fully understood his predicament but, as Bluff said, if Bruce could make a noise, he felt that would constitute a good part of the action.

The next morning the ponies entered the paddock and if Susan had been watching them closely, she would have noticed that Bluff had not played her up as much as usual. She put that down to the fact that he must have done a lot of pacing up and down in his stall the previous night, judging by the state of the bedding. As soon as they were on their own, Bluff drew up the battle plans and each pony was given an area to patrol. Don asked if it would interfere with his eating which received an instant rebuke from Bluff.

All that day, the ponies never left their allotted posts and a constant vigil was kept for any sign of Brer Fox. It was not until about 3.30 pm that a blood chilling whinny went up from Bobby, who was in the area next to the spinney. He was so excited that he could not get words out and he spluttered. The other ponies saw him, head down, going at great speed

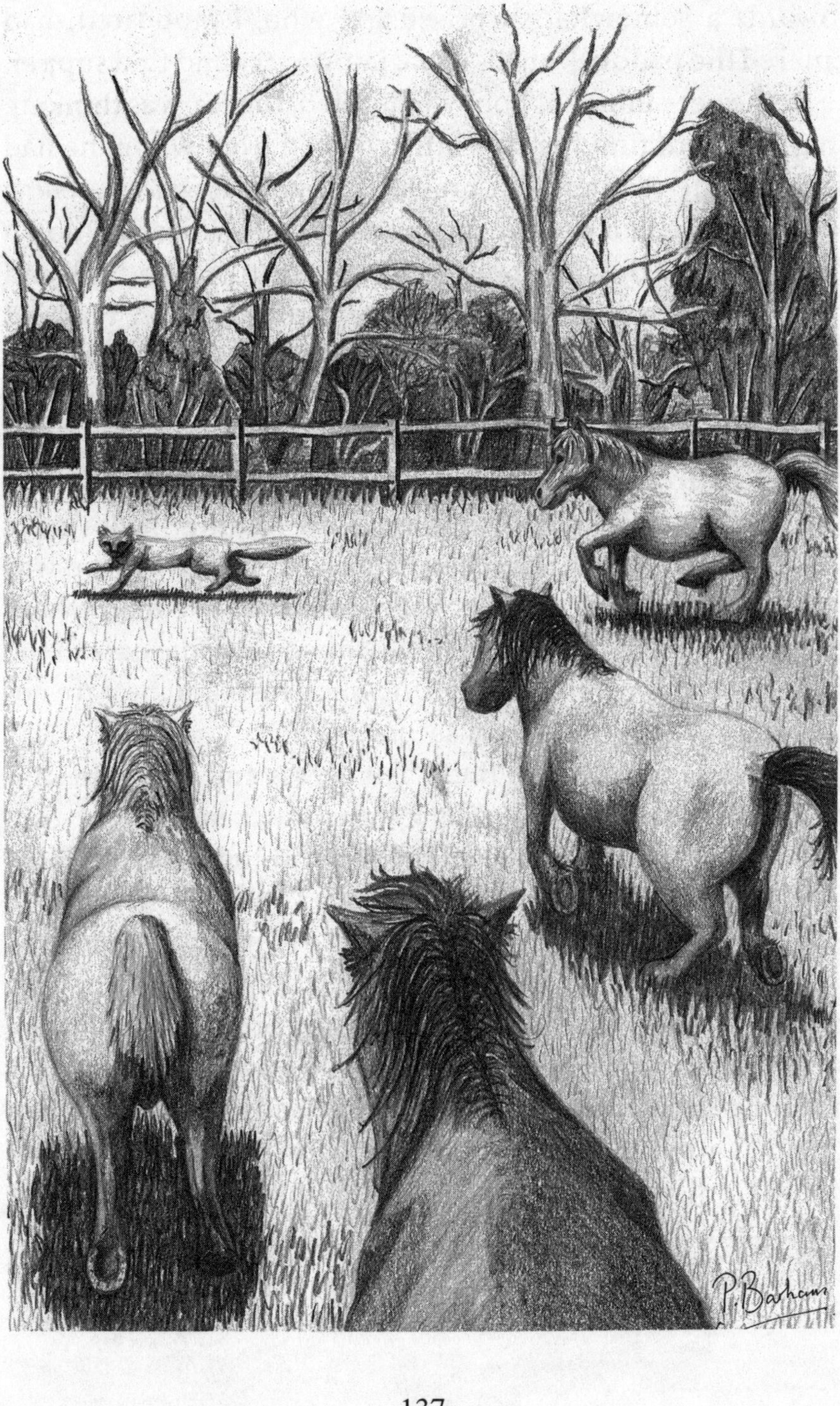

towards a somewhat surprised fox who, it appeared, had entered the paddock on his usual jaunt to try and find supper.

At the very moment Bobby whinnied, the fox was thinking that he might find the silly little chicken from whom he had grabbed the feathers the previous day. He was overcome with fright when he saw an enormous pony bearing down upon him. He did not know whether to run or stand still and hope the thing missed him. The fox was even more terrified when he looked around and saw two more ponies galloping towards him and another trotting as fast as he could, all shouting and whinnying and making a terrible row! In an instant he froze and the three fit ponies swooped down on him and he found he was faced with lashing heels and a swearing threesome, all telling him what a bounder he was and how they were going to kick him out of the field whenever he showed his ugly face! The fox squirmed closer to the fence. He had never seen such vicious beasts and he dare not take his eyes off them for a second.

"Quick Don" shouted Bluff "cut across and stop him slipping back into the spinney" and with a quick movement, Don was placing himself between the fox and the fence. The fox by now was beginning to wish he had not come out so early. Some of those hooves were pretty close to his head and it was not very nice. He made a dash between the two greys, hoping to out-run those old fellows. He caught Bruce and Bobby by surprise and slipped past. Bluff quickly saw the danger in his escaping and at a speed that even surprised him, he was in hot pursuit with Don and Bobby now making ground. For a small pony, Don could really travel and with the wind whistling through his mane, he enjoyed the chase immensely.

The fox kept running but with the sound of thundering hooves echoing in its ears, it veered suddenly to the left, hoping that the ponies would go straight on. He had not reckoned on the tenacity of Bluff who, seeing the turn, bent his body to go with the fox. Bobby with longer legs was cutting across the ground and Don was keeping up with Bluff. By this time, they were all winded and felt a sweat coming on but the speed was kept up.

The fox, using all his cunning, turned and twisted this way and that but he could not out-run those determined old ponies. The turf flew as they dug their hooves in to get a grip and although the fox mustered all his energies, it seemed that those four warriors from the pits matched him move for move.

Just as escape seemed impossible, the fox noticed the cows had started to run about so as to join in the excitement. With a final spurt, he made straight for them and passed between them, causing the pursuing ponies to swerve, or collide with the cows.

"Get out of the way you stupid things!" gasped Bluff but he knew that the fox had made good his escape and drew up, followed by a heaving Don and Bobby. Bruce trotted over and although he was not winded, he felt he had done his best.

"We showed that wretch, didn't we" cried a heaving Don, as he felt the adrenaline coursing through his veins.

"Of course we did" replied Bobby. "He was really worried and I bet it will be a long time before he sets foot anywhere near our paddock again!"

Bluff stood there. He just could not find the breath to reply. He was covered in sweat and it was then that he started to feel the effort of the chase catching up on him. "Whew" he thought "what a run!" and although his legs were shaking, he felt that it was well worth it, just for Cocky's sake.

When Susan came to collect them, she knew that they had

been running because one of the staff had seen them but she had no idea why. When she actually saw the state of them, she was most annoyed. Bluff, Don and Bobby were lathered up and she knew that if she did not get them into the stables quickly, rub them down and then rug them, they could be in for trouble. Bruce was all right. He was still grazing so Susan brought the other three in first and had assistance to get them dry and covered.

"What on earth have you all be doing?" she enquired, trying to think why three of the ponies would run for such a time to get into the state they were in. She mentioned the incident to Old Portly when he walked round but the mystery still remained. Had she known the reason, she would have been very proud of them for sticking up for the bantam, even though she knew that Cocky did not like her.

Bluff had his tea and immediately decided to stretch out. The exertions of the afternoon had been just a bit too much for him. After all, he thought to himself, I am not getting any younger.

"Are you lying down Bluff?" called Don, after he had finished searching the stall for any little titbit he might have missed at teatime.

"Yes" replied Bluff.

"I think I'll have a rest as well" went on Don, not wanting to be the first to lie down and be reminded of his age.

"Bobby's been down since just after Susan left" remarked Bruce who was still browsing through the hay nets. "In fact, he asked me to save his tea for him."

"Yes, and I bet you'll leave him a lot!" jeered Don, wishing he could be let loose with Bobby's tea for half an hour!

"Listen, fatty" snapped Bruce "not all of us are tarred in your colours!"

"What's that supposed to mean?" enquired Don all innocently.

"It means we are not all greedy like you" Bobby answered with a tired voice.

"Well if that is what it means, then why didn't he just say that instead of all that gibberish which I couldn't understand" said Don angrily.

"That's enough now" interjected Bluff. "Let's plan another campaign against that rotten fox."

"You really must be kidding" gasped Don, still feeling the drastic effects of the afternoon. "I have used up all my running capacity for at least the next six weeks and no way can my poor brain plan for another energy sapping venture, Cocky or no Cocky!"

"Thanks a lot" retorted Bluff, feeling somewhat let down by Don's refusal to plan further action in their fight for the other little animals which belonged to the Sanctuary.

"I never thought" he went on" I'd see the day when my old pal Don would jib away from a dust-up with anyone."

"Come off it" cried Don "this isn't a dust-up, it's a flipping vendetta and let's face it, none of us are the age for an ongoing battle with a fox who is fitter, younger, and may I add, craftier than we are!" Don felt that his answer was what was needed to let Bluff know that his days of being in charge were drawing to a close.

"Well, be that as it may" said a hurt Bluff "I for one will carry on this crusade until I know that poor little Cocky and his friends will be able to roam in this Sanctuary without any hindrance from some mangy fox!"

"Hear, hear" cried Bobby and Bruce hoped that he would not volunteer the both of them to a further adventure. Bruce wanted to side with Don in a way but he did not want to hurt

Bluff's feelings. He wanted to stay out of the conversation but here was his brother, Bobby, getting all patriotic again and that spelt danger.

"Are you ready to continue?" enquired Bluff of Bobby.

"Yes I am" replied Bobby stoutly "I will never have anyone say that I let them down. Justice is justice and I am sure that if Bruce were fit, he would join me in that sentiment."

"Oh I would, I would" put in Bruce, grateful to be getting out of this predicament as lightly as that.

"So you see Don" said the confident Bluff "the two greys do not share your pessimism and cowardly attitude."

"Cowardly" snorted Don "there's nothing cowardly in what I said. It was all common sense!" Now it was Don's turn to feel hurt and Bruce thought it a much better idea to try and let the conversation go. Bluff had already decided that he would stand and plan the next move quietly.

The fox never appeared the next day but just after dinner the three little girls started calling and seeing as Bluff and Bobby were all for a little light refreshment and having, as Bluff said "..no principles about being ridden.." they went over to them and spent an hour enjoying the offerings and in return paying them back by gently walking up and down. Don was furious and he kept about twenty yards clear of them, marching back and forth, throwing his head in the air with disgust and jealousy.

As soon as Susan had served tea that day a fluttering at Bluff's door meant that Cocky was back AND in action.

"Did you all hear about my skirmish with the fox?" he asked.

Bluff told him what they knew of the incident, hoping that Cocky would tell them some more - if there was any more to tell. "He wasn't half big" went on Cocky indicating with his wings some idea of the size of his assailant "and ugly. Why, do you know, he was even more ugly than you, and that's saying something!"

"Now just you hang on a minute" interrupted Don "nobody's going to call me ugly."

"Oh, don't be so sensitive" Cocky continued. "What you've got to remember is that an animal like you is ugly compared with a thing of beauty like me!" and with that, all the stalls erupted either with snorts or laughter.

"He is serious you know" said Don.

"Of course I am serious" said a very angry bantam. "You all know full well that I am prettier than the lot of you, don't you?" and the ponies realised that the little bird was not joking, he was really serious.

"Well, now you've told us how beautiful you are" put in Bruce "maybe you'd like to carry on telling us about this enormous fox who nearly had you for supper."

"Oh, do shut up" snapped Cocky "you send a shiver through my feathers just thinking about that horrible thing."

"Well, come on" said Don impatiently "tell us what happened."

"Well, it was like this" started Cocky "I was having a look through some dead leaves that the bald-headed gardener had left in a pile, when out of nowhere, somebody or something takes a grab at m'rear feathers! Well, I'm not kidding. I leapt all of ten feet in the air and it was only then that I noticed this evil looking creature with half m'backside hanging from his mouth. I can tell you lot, I nearly fainted with fright and ran like hell. Of course, this wicked brute gives chase doesn't he and believe me, I had visions of not being around anymore. Suddenly from out of nowhere comes the gardener fella actually running AND let me say how glad I was to see him, even if me and him don't really get on like.." Cocky paused. The mere thought of the whole episode had brought him out in a cold sweat.

"Was the fox very far away from you?" enquired Bobby.

"Far away?" cried Cocky "he was that close I could feel his hot breath on me bare backside. In a way, I suppose every time I see the gardener, I will have to feel grateful to him - even when he chases me off his garden with his hoe!"

All the ponies, including Don, had listened to Cocky with pictures flashing through their minds of the evil fox chasing the poor little innocent bantam through the Sanctuary. Had the gardener not arrived in time then Cocky would have been, as Don said "a goner!"

"There you are" said Bluff "how could any of you not want to carry on the fight against this terrible predator when you look at this poor defenceless creature up in the roof!"

"Hang on a bit" cooed Cocky "I'm not that defenceless you know. Remember, it was me who took on the humans when they had that ceremony thing - and I won!" he reminded them. "So don't think that I can't look after m'self."

"What then would have happened if Bill the gardener had not arrived at the opportune time?" asked Bluff with more than a shade of sarcasm in his voice ". You know, when the fox was just about to get his teeth into more than your feathers!"

(Gulp),"I never thought of that.." Cocky owned up. "When you put it like that, I am a poor little defenceless creature - very beautiful of course!"

"Did you hear that?" snorted Don "flipping conceited to the end."

"Why not?" remarked Cocky "if you've got beauty and charisma, why not publicise it. The trouble with you, Don, you just happen to be thick AND ugly which is not an ideal combination."

"Why, you over-blown sparrow!" snarled Don, feeling that he had been outwitted by that 'creature' in the roof.

"Sticks and stones may break my bones but names will never hurt me" sang Cocky from his perch, well out of harms way.

"If I get my hooves anywhere near to you, I'll, I'll, flipping hurt you" shouted the angry Don.

"Now then you two!" interjected Bluff. " That's enough! Let me tell you, Cocky, that Don really went for that fox yesterday and so did the others so you should thank them."

"I never realised" apologised Cocky "that my good friends the ponies would ever take my part in a fight, especially old thicky!"

"I won't do it again" promised Don. "It will be you that I chase and woe betide you if I catch you."

"YOU catch me?" Cocky screeched. "You would have to get up early in the morning to do that, especially carrying the weight you do!"

Don spluttered and snorted. He really loathed the bantam and Bluff thought it wise not to say any more.

After a while, the stables fell into a silence which meant that all had been said that was going to be said that evening and the ponies settled down for the night.

Chapter 15

Aghast in the Gorse

As the winter continued the days grew shorter and shorter. The ponies spent a lot more time in the stables. This was not to their liking but with the frost on the grass nearly every day, Susan was only able to put them out for short periods. Even when the snow lay on the ground their adventures were limited to short exercise runs.

None of them liked this time of year and even Cocky was going to roost more and more in the hen house because it was warmer. Besides, he told them, there was a new little hen to whom he felt he should be introduced - so the stables took second place.

Apart from occasional visits from the vet and the farrier, life for the ponies was pretty uneventful. The three little girls did not visit them so often, although Bluff said he often heard them laughing as they played in the snow. Susan came to work when it was dark and went home when it was dark and life was pretty boring for the four friends left so long in their stalls.

All the ponies looked forward to when the season changed and it was uncanny the way they knew when that change was about to take place. It all happened one day when the birds changed their song; the humans would not have noticed it so much but the ponies and all the other animals sensed it immediately. Looking out of their stalls, Bluff and the greys could see across the Sanctuary, the snowdrops beginning to appear and daffodils were beginning to shoot up which meant that it would not be long before they burst into flower. They felt the change in their bones and soon they would be able to spend longer and longer in the fields. For many months, visitors to the Sanctuary had been few but with the coming of spring, they would return and that meant one thing to Don - "treats!"

Looking out in the morning light, the ponies could see all the small animals scratching in the grounds and it was as if they witnessed a new world rather than a season change.

One afternoon, after they had finished their tea the familiar flutterings told them that their old friend, Cocky Bantam, had come back.

"What-ho me old mates" he cackled. "How have you been? I hope you have missed me."

"I haven't" snorted Don, still thinking of their last encounter.

"I didn't expect you to, misery" he bounced back "but I bet the others have, haven't you mates?"

"Well, it has been rather quiet" admitted Bluff, not wanting Cocky to get a bigger head than he already had.

"I bet old Miss Prim thought she had got rid of me from the stables" Cocky went on "but you see fellas, like a bad penny, here I am!"

"We heard you had found another lady friend" said Bobby "what happened, we haven't seen you with her at all."

"We won't go into that" said Cocky with a matter of fact air "some things are best unspoken."

"What do you mean? She rumbled you?" asked Don, putting his oar in when he could.

"What do you mean 'rumbled' me?" enquired Cocky, trying to sound all innocent.

"I mean she flipping found you out to be what you really are" Don went on.

"Oh, you mean handsome, intelligent and agile!" Cocky teased, knowing full well that it would draw the worst out of the small black pony.

"I mean" spluttered Don, getting really up-tight "she found out that you are big headed, self opinionated and flipping rude!"

"Well, let's say we had a slight difference of opinion" agreed Cocky "but nothing that I couldn't have put right, had I wanted to ..." and to this Don just stamped his hoof.

It was during the winter that Mr. Harry, the vet, had informed the Captain that in order to keep Don fit and his laminitis in check, it would be advisable to build a small enclosed paddock so that he could not eat too much grass.

The small paddock had been erected. It meant that with the rich spring grass now available, Don would be able to stay out all day but not eat too much and thus not aggravate his problem. The other ponies were better and only Bluff had a time limit on him. He would be brought in at four thirty rather than stay out for the whole of the twenty four hours. The greys' condition was such that the vet thought that as soon as the climate permitted, there would be no reason for them to come in each day and in that way, he hoped that they would build themselves up, ready for the next winter.

Don had no idea that he was going to be treated any differently from his three friends and Susan was a little apprehensive at what he would do once he found out. As for the greys, she decided that they would follow the same pattern as Bluff for the time being as, in her opinion, the weather was not yet warm enough for them to be out the whole time.

On the fateful morning when the ponies started their new routine, two things happened. One was that Don would take up his new residence for the danger months. The second that the other ponies would only graze one half of the paddock as the other half was to be left for the Captain to hold his Annual Gala on that field in July.

Susan placed Bluff and the greys out in their half of the paddock first and everything went well. Then it was Don's turn. He was quite happy until the "stupid wench" turned right instead of left and that took him into a "...tin pot piece of the field.." as quoted by Don later that evening "...not sufficient to graze a rabbit."

As Susan went to take his halter off, Don became rather abusive and although Susan and anyone else could not understand what was being uttered by a very upset old pony, nevertheless his three companions and the cows understood every word and it was not language that was printable. "YOU STUPID, FUNNY LOOKING OLD B....." Don shouted at poor Susan "What the hell are you doing-shoving me in this excuse for a paddock. I demand to be placed in the proper field with my friends."

Of course, Susan could not understand one word of the tirade from a very cross pony but the way he tossed his head and stamped his feet gave her the impression that he was not exactly in love with his new surroundings. Try as she may, he would not stay still long enough for her to remove his halter. In desperation she left it on. Then came the tricky bit of trying to get out of the gate. Don just would not let her. As soon as the poor girl reached the gate and tried to squeeze through and close it again, he pushed all his weight and twice he nearly squashed her.

As a last ditch stand, she closed the gate from inside and

went to climb over it but that was her undoing. Just as she hooked her leg over the bar, her weight was then unevenly distributed for a split second. Instantly, Don reared his head under her and pushed the poor unfortunate girl. She flew over the gate and went head first into some gorse bushes! She shouted at Don and called him everything. She concluded by saying "I'll never forgive you for that..." and stormed away, her face and hands bleeding and grazed from the gorse. The commotion had brought the other ponies and the cows up to the fence to see what was happening.

Although Bluff felt sorry for Susan, he could not stop laughing when he saw Don catch her with his head, just as she was getting over the fence. He must have lifted her at least two feet clear of the top rail, head first and Bluff winced as he heard her thump on to the ground. He had to look away when the poor girl used language that Bluff did not even know she knew! He had heard the pitmen say words like that but never a fair-haired, nice gentle looking girl like Susan. He was surprised to say the least!

"Did you see that then?" Don shouted across. "What a flyer she took. I bet she doesn't tell Old Portly. It must rate as my best effort since you bit her backside!"

The other animals all rocked with mirth and the cows who had no feelings for Susan anyway, always supported the ponies in their arguments with humans. They thought Don's lift was marvellous.

"Have you seen the size of this prison that wretched girl has put me in?" enquired Don, returning to serious matters. "I bet none of you would like it. There's not even enough grass in here to keep a mouse alive!"

"I didn't think mice ate grass" suggested Bobby, not foreseeing that a remark like that was just what Don did not need.

The reply was exactly what the grey should have expected. "You stupid oaf" roared Don "I didn't mean that literally, it was just a figure of speech."

"What is a figure of speech?" the puzzled Bobby asked, quite unaware of the insults hurled at him.

"Oh, shut up and get back to your knitting!" yelled Don.

"What's that?" he was asked and as Don did not know, he turned and trotted to the other end of his stamp-sized cage.

Bruce noted that with them only having half the normal paddocks, it could cause some problems with the cows who were not the best animals to share a paddock with. Bluff merely said they would have to be strict and demand their share of the grazing. After all, the grass was growing quite well.

"Yes" said Bruce "but have you seen the way they eat it? Anyone would think they have never tasted fresh grass before."

"Be that as it may" replied Bluff "we will have to lay the law down to them and make sure that we get our fair share. After all, we live here - they are only guests."

"I've been thinking" chipped in Bobby "what did Don mean about a figure of speech?" As the other ponies did not know and what was more, did not care, neither of them bothered to answer which left Bobby more perplexed than ever.

The next piece of excitement was when Susan came to fetch Don in from his small paddock and the black pony definitely did not see the funny side of it. He considered that he had been downgraded enough already and was not going to let her embarrass him further by bringing him in any earlier than the others. So, as she entered the gate, he trotted to the other end and waited. Susan advanced on him with a meaningful

151

look in her eye. She was still smarting from his earlier attack. As she approached, the little devil reared on his hind feet and menaced the poor girl who quickly jumped out of the way.

"Now come on Don. I don't want any more trouble from you" she said.

"Trouble? You've not had any trouble yet, you stupid biddy. I'll teach you to treat me differently from the others."

With that, he reared again but this time Susan did not jump out of the way. She moved sideways and dug him in the ribs as he passed. It took the wind out of his sails for a moment and he faltered.

"You are spiteful" he snorted as he prepared to rear again and once more Susan caught him exactly in the right spot. "Hang on a minute" he gasped as her actions took his breath away "there's no need to become your usual vicious self" and for a brief time he calmed down, not really knowing how to combat someone who seemed to delight in making him feel small. Don was in a dilemma. He did not want to be seen to be giving in to the girl but on the other hand, he was not too happy about the way she dug him in the tummy each time he reared at her.

Susan felt that she was winning and started to lead the black pony out of the paddock when suddenly Don stopped and refused to move. He knew that he would most probably get into trouble so he decided that it would be a token gesture -just to let her know that he was not going to be bossed around all the time. Eventually, Susan managed to lead Don into the stable. He had a hard time controlling his anger because every time she turned her back on him, she could feel him turn. He was waiting for the right opportunity to get his own back on her. She was still sore from the lift over the gate he had given her. So both the pony and girl played a cat and mouse game, neither trusting the other in the slightest.

The daily battle went on and on. Don hated going into his 'cage' each day, mainly because what little grass had been there, he had devoured in the first couple of mornings. As he was first and foremost a greedy animal, it meant starvation to him and he was prepared to fight tooth and nail for his stomach. Susan was worn down to tears by his actions and the constant wariness of being on her guard against him, took its toll. Many a time, when she was on her own, she often burst into tears. At one stage, she was on the brink of asking Old Portly if she could be removed from her duty with the ponies to look after some other animals, but her love for them changed her mind and she decided that she would play Don's game. In front of him, she appeared very strong and defiant which did not go down at all well with Don who told the others that in his opinion he thought she was a wicked wretch. When none of his friends agreed with him, he sulked for days.

Chapter 16

A Wetting for Bluff

Meanwhile the other ponies were having their problems with the cows who, for some reason, would not co-operate over the grazing. As it was Bluff who took it into his head to admonish them, they took a violent dislike to him. If he was busy grazing, they would deliberately stand in his way, making him move to another spot and then they would follow him, making life difficult for him.

As for the greys, they hardly complained to the cows so they were left alone most of the time. The cows made fun of Bobby because they thought he was 'funny.' Bobby took no notice and both he and Bruce carried on as though they never existed; so it meant that all their spite had to be taken out on Bluff. It was at times like these that he missed Don for support. After all, it did not matter what faults he had, Don always joined with Bluff and if anyone picked on Bluff, they also picked on Don. Alas, Don was separated and that left the old warrior on his own.

It was due to this trouble that an event took place which nearly saw the last of Bluff and caused the cows to be moved from the paddock. It happened one morning at about ten thirty. Bluff was making his way across the paddock to the drinking trough which was situated halfway across the dividing fence between the paddock they were using, and the one that was presently fallow. Bluff noticed one of the cows grazing close by the trough so he took his time and although very thirsty, felt it better to let the cow move away before going to drink. As the cow cleared the area, Bluff moved in and having a look round, saw that it was clear for him to drink.

The old pony drank long and deep at the water trough and had no thoughts much in his head, except for the fact that he loved it at the Sanctuary. Having finished, Bluff turned to walk away when he saw one of the cows standing there right beside him.

He had been so absorbed in what he had been doing, he had not heard the cow approach. Bluff thought nothing of it and turned to leave. Just then, the cow lowered its head and caught Bluff in the stomach just as the pony had shifted his balance. Without anything to stop him, Bluff fell sideways into the trough which was a long galvanised one, with a dividing rod half way for added strength. The old pony's rear end was in one side of the trough and his shoulders in the other. Despite his struggles, there he was, stuck fast with his body immersed in the water and his feet off the ground. He had no leverage to free himself and with his head hanging over the end of the trough, he felt as though it was going to fall off.

The offending cow just stood and gloated over her actions and the two greys almost went into a frenzy. What could they do? Bruce suggested that they went over and cleared the cows away to avoid them doing any more damage to Bluff but apart from that there was nothing they could do except hope that one of the humans would come out and see the poor old fellow stuck, helpless in the water.

After what seemed an eternity, a lady came down to look into the paddock to see 'the dear old ponies from the pits...' At first, she could not believe her eyes when she saw one of them taking a bath (as she thought) and after a minute or two slowly strolled up to the office to thank the girl there for letting her go and see them. As she came out of the office, she casually mentioned the fact that it was unusual to see a pony having a bath in a water trough and left. It was seconds before what she had said permeated through to the girl on duty.

"A bath in the water trough? Oh my God, what has happened?" she wondered as she flew through the door and down towards the paddocks. Susan was just walking up after cleaning the stables and clearing up.

"Quick Susan" the girl shouted "the ponies! Something terrible is happening!"

"What are you talking about" asked Susan as she turned to run towards the field with the girl.

"I don't know for sure" the girl gasped "but an old lady said one was having a bath in the trough!"

"Oh, no!" echoed Susan and ran as fast as she could. The sight that met their eyes was unbelievable. There was poor Bluff, well and truly stuck and visibly getting weaker.

"Oh for God's sake get the Manager" Susan cried and the girl ran back with her lungs bursting to get help. Every member of staff she met on the way was told to get down to the paddock to help Susan. When the girl found the Manager, Old Portly, she had a job to get her words out.

"What?" he roared.

"It's Bluff" the girl panted "he's in a bad way in the water trough."

"What do you mean girl?" he asked.

"Bluff has fallen into the water trough" explained the girl "and Susan needs help badly." Without more ado, the Manager charged into the office and dialled for the Fire Brigade

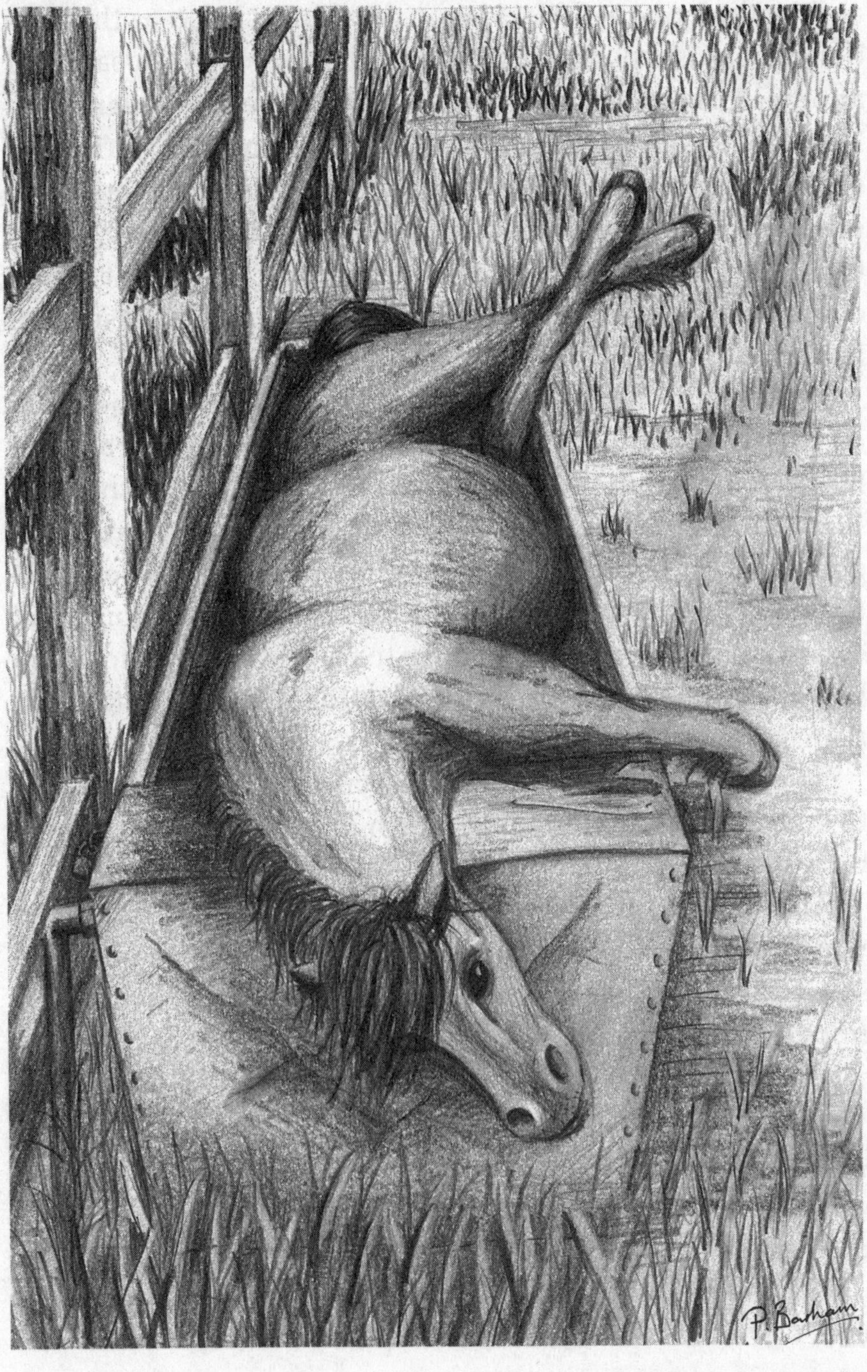
P. Barham

and he then phoned Mr. Harry, the vet. As soon as this was done, he rushed down to the paddock where Susan and another girl were supporting the pony's head in their arms. Now and again, Bluff tried to struggle free but the staff could see that he was getting weaker; the supporting rod across the centre of the trough was cutting into him with every move. Old Portly told the girls to get bales of straw so that Susan could support his head, thus taking some of the pressure off her arms.

All this time, Bluff was feeling waves of agony as the throb increased and although the feeling of Susan's arms around his neck helped, it did not stop the red mist of pain that was spreading across his body. Bluff wanted to carry on struggling because his natural instincts told him he must do something to ease the situation. He knew that if Susan could not do anything, then he would have to try and hold out for extra help to arrive, or, as he knew, he would not be able to take the pain any more.

"We must have help soon" Susan cried. "He will not be able to take the pressure on his stomach much longer" and it was then she noticed that Bluff's eyes had started to roll.

All eyes and ears were turned towards the direction in which the Fire Brigade would come. Every person at the scene of the disaster was willing them to get there quickly. "I hope the vet arrives here soon" said Old Portly to Susan, who was arranging the straw bales to help support Bluff's head. The pony started to snort and his efforts to free himself became more feeble as the seconds ticked by. A faint siren caught their ears and a few sighs were heard as help seemed real at last. The noise grew louder and Old Portly delegated one of the girls to run up the drive to tell the firemen where they were. Another was asked to open the main gate and then stand by to stop the other animals from getting out of the paddock.

The Fire Brigade came rushing up. The cows thought this was a great game and decided to have a gallop around the field, adding to the confusion that was already reigning there. Just behind the Fire Brigade was a smaller vehicle with "RESCUE" boldly printed on the side and it appeared that those men were experts on trapped animals. The water was disconnected from the mains and the pipe leading to the trough quickly unscrewed after which the men lost no time in trying to rescue Bluff.

Mr. Harry arrived and had a quick look at the old pony. "I think we will have to work fast " he said to Susan "he seems to be slipping." He took a syringe from his bag and prepared to give Bluff an injection to help him.

"Does it look bad?" enquired Susan with a note of weariness in her voice.

"I'm afraid it does" replied the vet. "It is surprising that he has lasted so long. He must be a strong old pony."

"Oh, he is" agreed Susan. "He loves life and will fight every inch of the way."

"Well, that will help" said Mr. Harry. The firemen took crowbars from their vehicle and lined up on one side of the trough.

"When I say lift" said the Leading Fireman "I want you all to lift together" and the men prepared themselves for the weight that they knew they would have to lift.

"He must weigh over a ton" remarked one of the firemen.

"I bet you're right there" stated another.

"Ready men? Now LIFT" and the muscles of the men rippled as they took the strain. The contortions of their faces showed how heavy Bluff was and how tight the trough had been secured to the ground. To upset their rhythm Bluff decided to have a final fling and his struggling placed an extra burden on the firemen, now joined by members of the staff.

Mr. Harry helped Susan to comfort the pony and by looking at him, the vet knew that the strain was gradually becoming too much for Bluff.

"Come on my lads, one final heave" called the Leading Fireman and the grunts coming from the line of crowbars told how much effort was being put in on behalf of Bluff.

"One more try..." came the yell. With superhuman strength the firemen tilted the trough over and the water under Bluff started to spill out.

"Keep it up lads" called the leader and slowly they felt their efforts paying off. The trough was beginning to ease off its base and then, with one final heave, Bluff was shot from his watery prison and on to the grass. There was water everywhere. Mr. Harry and Susan took the most of it and both were absolutely soaked. Bluff lay still. He did not really know what had happened to him but he knew the pain was going and then he felt himself passing out. "Quickly Susan" called Mr. Harry. "Keep his head up and talk to him so that you have contact."

Mr. Harry took out his stethoscope from his bag and placed it on the old pony's heart. From what he heard, he knew that he had to give Bluff a stimulant and reached again into his bag.

All the firemen stood around and the sweat on their faces showed just how hard they had strained to get the old fellow free.

"Is he going to be all right?" asked one, with tears in his eyes.

"It's a bit early" said Mr. Harry "but as he is a fighter there is always a chance."

As Bluff lay still, only the soft words from Susan could be heard as she pleaded with him to hang on and fight. The other ponies were kept well away and were most anxious to know what had happened to their friend. Even Don in his 'cage' across the paddock paced up and down urging his pal to get up so that he could see that he was all right.

"How in the world did the pony get in the trough?" asked the Leading Fireman and the only animals who could have explained the circumstances were making a nuisance of themselves over by the gate.

"No one knows the answer to that question" interjected Old Portly "and maybe we will never know what happened."

The vet was massaging Bluff and every now and then he stopped to listen to his heart. It was touch and go. No one knew more than Mr. Harry what the staff would be feeling if they lost Bluff. For all his faults, he was, thought Mr. Harry, the undisputed leader of the group.

"Imagine" said another fireman "he worked all those years underground and survived roof falls, knocks and bruises and to be put out by water, it wouldn't be right would it?" and the shaking of heads told him that all his colleagues agreed.

"Come on lads, let's get this lot sorted out." The authoritative voice of the Leading Fireman brought them all back to the task in hand. He wanted to keep his men busy. He did not want them to join the Sanctuary staff in mourning the old pony before he had gone.

To Bluff, the first thing he remembered was Susan's voice saying "Come on, you silly old thing! You've had worse troubles than this!"

He wondered "who is she calling 'silly'" and his head started to clear. Mr. Harry touched Susan's sleeve: "I think we've got the old boy" he said. "I am getting a stronger pulse at last." Susan looked up and choked back her emotion.

"Come on Bluff" she whispered. "You will be all right now" and very slowly the pony began to stir.

"Keep talking to him" Mr. Harry told Susan. "It is your voice that he is clinging to." So Susan kept whispering very softly.

Bluff thought that she was at the end of a long tunnel, just like they had down in the mine and he could see some daylight at the end of it. "Maybe I am back in the pit" he thought, but no, it was Susan's voice all right. He wanted to shout "Where are you?" to her but he could not. "Keep on talking" he wanted to say but somehow he was not saying anything.

Mr. Harry was now smiling and he looked up to the anxious faces all around him and said: "Susan's voice has brought Bluff back and now all we have to do is to hold on to him."

"Do you think she can keep him getting stronger?" asked Old Portly and the vet explained that apart from some freak accident between where they stood and when Bluff gained all his senses, the pony should be all right.

"I'll stay with him" he said and the other staff started drifting away to look after the animals they were responsible for in the Sanctuary.

Susan looked up. Coming across the paddock from the direction of the lane was a little grey-haired old lady. At first she thought it might be someone just coming to have a look but by the way the person was waving a stick, she knew there was more to her visit than pure inquisitiveness.

"I saw it all" the old lady was saying. "I am a witness to it" she went on. Mr. Harry stood up.

"I beg your pardon Madam?" he queried.

"I saw the whole thing" replied the lady, getting very excited.

"Saw what?" enquired the vet.

"That big black and white cow push the horse into the water" she explained. "I saw it happen."

"Tell me what you saw again" questioned Mr. Harry, wanting to find out just what the lady saw. "I was walking down the lane" the lady went on "and I saw that poor horse standing by the trough drinking and that black and white cow went up and as soon as the horse turned to walk away, the cow deliberately went up and butted him with its head. At first, I didn't think much about it and thought they were playing, so you can imagine my surprise when I came back from the shops and saw all of you out here and him, bless him, stretched out on the ground."

"You actually saw a cow go up to the pony and butt him into the trough?" Mr. Harry just HAD to clarify with her again.

"Yes, of course I did! I said so didn't I?" The old lady was quite indignant.

"It's not that I disbelieved you" went on Mr. Harry "I just wanted to make sure that I heard you correctly."

"You did!" said the little old lady, rising up to all of her five foot two. "You did!"

"Well, thank you very much for coming forward" said the vet. "You've been very helpful."

"Is he going to be all right then?"

"Yes, I think so" replied the vet reassuringly, "and thank you, once again."

"You're welcome" said the dear old lady and she started to walk back the same way she had come.

"Well, that solves that mystery!" said the vet. "We will have to have the cows moved out of the paddocks, just in case it happens again."

"I don't think I could stand it again" remarked Susan "What with Bruce having the roof fall on him and now this. Whew, it's all too much."

"Well Susan! You know what they say 'Everything is sent to try us'" went on Mr. Harry.

"That's all very well" replied the girl "but I don't like being tried."

Bluff was still in his tunnel but the daylight was getting nearer and he could hear the voices much plainer now, especially Susan's. He thought he heard her laugh but could not be sure. Don was still impatiently waiting to hear how bad his friend was and having Susan and the wretched vet with Bluff all the time did not help the black pony to calm down. "Goodness knows what that terrible couple will do to him" he thought and then he decided he would take time to scavenge a few blades of grass that were left in his 'hell hole.'

The greys had been kept back from the area along with the cows. The ponies knew what had happened so naturally they ignored the cows. They both vowed they would get even for what had been done to one of the nicest ponies they had ever known. For a while neither of them could comprehend what was going on with Bluff except that they knew with Susan holding him so long, it had to be serious.

"Oh, I do hope he's all right" whimpered Bobby.

"So do I" agreed Bruce. "Why, oh why, did those horrible things have to go and do a thing like this?"

"It was because Bluff told them a thing or two.." retorted Bobby.

"That may be so" went on Bruce "but we could have stood

up to them more than we did you know."

"Yes, I thought that too" Bobby had to admit. "In future" he declared "I will stand by old Bluff come hell or high water."

Bruce looked startled: "Where on earth did you learn that saying?" he asked.

"Oh, I don't know" remarked Bobby. "It just seemed to be apt for the occasion."

Bluff opened his eyes and through a blur saw Susan. He was so thrilled; he could not think of a better sight to see at such a time.

"Hello Bluff" she said and planted a big kiss right on the end of his nose. "I'm glad you are back; you had me worried at one time."

"Had you worried" thought Bluff. "How do you think I felt!" He gave a little snort and the vet thought that was a very encouraging sign. After a short while Mr. Harry suggested that Susan should see if the pony could stand. Mr. Harry explained that he wanted to check if anything was broken or not. Susan stood up and instinctively Bluff hauled himself off the ground. He was very unsteady at first but as the dizziness wore off, he felt more like his old self. He had an enormous headache from holding his head up for so long but he was able to nuzzle Susan and when the other ponies saw him on his feet, they were all relieved and glad. Don was thrilled. Susan slowly walked the old fellow back to the stables. He was a little tottery but Mr. Harry declared that there were no breakages and he would be as good as new in no time.

As they passed Don's small paddock, the vet went over to where the black pony stood and in a friendly way, went to stroke his nose. Don was having none of that. He merely tossed his head and walked away as though to say "push off."

"Not very friendly" said the vet and Susan who had already passed, looked around and said: "You can say that again! He HATES that paddock!"

"Well" said Mr. Harry "if he is to survive that's where he will have to stay until the beginning of July."

"That's all right" replied Susan "but try telling him that!"

The firemen cleared up their equipment and replaced the trough and the fence and as soon as they had made sure everything was in order, they left. All the people and animals at the Sanctuary would be eternally grateful for their speed in responding to the call to help Bluff and as the vet said, it was most probably their quick action that had saved the poor old pony's life.

Before they left the Sanctuary, Old Portly had invited them to the Gala Day and asked them to bring a display to show the public the Fire Brigade's work not only with people, but also with animals as well.

Mr. Harry telephoned the Captain to arrange the removal of the cows who, he said, could cause even more damage to the ponies now that a vendetta had been uncovered. The Captain said he would send a cattle truck to pick them up that day as he needed cattle at one of his other sanctuaries.

That evening, as soon as the staff had gone, Cocky Bantam flew up on to Bluff's door and enquired:

"Are you all right mate?" in a very nice, soft, caring voice. Bluff liked that.

"Yes Cocky, I'm feeling much better now, thank you very much."

"I'm glad" said the bantam. "If it had been old grumpy next door, I would have expected it, but not you me old mate, not you.."

"That's nice of you to say so" replied Bluff.

"I don't think that was nice of him at all" Don called out.

"Why should I have been more likely to go in the drink than Bluff?"

"Because you are so blooming miserable and spiteful" snapped Cocky.

"Oh, thank you friend" Don hit back sarcastically.

"Well, it's true" continued Cocky. "Look at the life you are giving Susan at the moment. I don't like her a lot but I certainly wouldn't give her the hell that you are."

"What about the life she's giving me?" shouted Don. "Don't feel sorry for me, will you!"

"Oh, please don't start fighting again" interjected Bobby whose nerves were still recovering from the day's events.

"All right" replied Cocky. "I will ignore the little fat one."

"Watch it!" growled Don. "Just watch it!"

"Or what?" asked Cocky fluttering up to the safety of the roof. Don ignored him. "I'm glad the cows are gone" Cocky said to Bluff. "Things were getting a little naughty out there and anything could have happened."

"Yes, they could" agreed Bluff, "but I never dreamt that they would do such a mean and spiteful thing over hardly anything" he went on. "After all, I was only looking after their welfare as well as ours."

"Yes" continued Cocky, "but they didn't want you looking after their welfare as well, did they?"

"Well, that's how it seems now" concluded Bluff.

"It's good riddance to them, that's all I can say" Bobby chirped up. "I am sure we won't miss them."

"That's a point" said Cocky.

"I thought that Susan and Mr. Harry were marvellous" put in Bruce. "The way they stayed with you, Bluff, and never once stood up or left you..."

"I know" said Bluff. "It was Susan's voice which came

through like a dream that kept me going."

"It would have been more like a flipping nightmare had it been me.." cried Don, hoping to deflect some of the hero-worship away from Susan.

"That is what I call utter rudeness" remonstrated Bluff to Don. "When you are in a bad way like that, you need all the help and comfort you can get."

"If it had been Don, I reckon Susan and the vet would have got up and walked away" said Cocky "the only help to hand would have been Old Portly and you know the type of help he would give!"

"Did Susan give you the kiss of life?" asked Bobby.

"If she had" quipped Don "he would have been poisoned by now!"

"Oh, do be quiet Don!" said Bluff. "If you can't say anything nice, don't say anything." Don took the hint and dozed off.

Apart from aches and pains and stiffness in his joints, the following day found Bluff almost back to normal and this pleased all his friends. He noticed that when he was slowly led out to the paddocks most of the small animals like the chickens and bantams lined up to see him and as he passed, they all wished him well. Bluff enjoyed the fuss. He was a bit of a showman at heart, despite his facade of being beyond all the adulation. He felt quite important as he made his way to the field. He passed Don in his little paddock but when he looked over to pass the time of day, he noticed that Don was busily rooting around to find food. The greys were at the gate and Bobby suggested a little gallop. Bruce immediately rebuked him - the very suggestion, to say the least, was a little stupid. Bobby took it all in good part and merely put his nose to the ground and wandered off, pretending not to care.

Underneath Bobby was hurt because he thought he was just being friendly.

The smell of the grass filled Bluff's nostrils and to think if things had not been successful yesterday, he would not have been experiencing this pleasure. He glanced across at the water trough which the day before had been panic and confusion. Today, it stood as it always had to serve a purpose.

The serenity of the scene made an impression on the old pony. He was glad that he did not have to fight the cows any more and felt secure in that knowledge. Bluff lifted his nose to the air and breathed in the sweetness. He was so happy to live there.

Chapter 17

Dental Parade

Over the next few weeks, life for the ponies settled down into a comfortable routine. It was Susan, however, who noticed that the two greys and Bluff were not eating their grass properly. As they munched, balls of grass were falling from their mouths unchewed.

She reported her observation to Mr. Harry who said he would come down and give them a dental check-up.

Bluff was first in the dental line-up and when he had his mouth opened he shook his head a bit. He was not too sure what Mr. Harry was going to do! Susan held the old pony and the vet produced a long file from his bag and started to file the rear teeth. Bluff nearly leaped through the ceiling. As the rasp went to and fro, he thought his head was coming off and the vibrations of it echoed right through his brain. "Wow" he thought "I'm not having that" and Susan had a difficult time trying to hold him. Fortunately for Bluff, his teeth were not too bad and it was soon over. He raced around the field a bit still with the feeling of the rasp going through his skull. It was awful.

Mr. Harry decided to have both Bruce and Bobby brought in next from the field. They were to have an examination only because he considered that if their teeth were that bad, he would have to seek help from his colleague, Mr. David. Both the greys were examined and it was found that their rear grinding teeth required attention. Mr. Harry explained to

Susan that instead of the crown of the teeth being flat and able to grind up the grass, they were worn on one side and that meant the teeth went up to a point stopping the ponies from chewing their food. This in turn would cause tummy problems and they could lose weight. He said that it hurt them and stopped them from eating. Susan asked how urgent was the problem and Mr. Harry replied that they would have a go at them the next day.

Bluff never told his friends about the teeth treatment except to say that it was not a comfortable feeling and left it at that. The next day when Bobby was brought in from the field he was not exactly worried about having his teeth seen to. The vets had chosen a nice smooth patch of lawn and assembled some of the staff. Mr. David explained to them what he was going to do. He would put loops of rope around the feet of the pony and then place a rope through these and when they were pulled tight, the pony would go down on the grass and then he would secure them off and the job would begin. Placing the loops around Bobby's feet went quite well but as soon as the rope was put in place and pulled, all hell was let loose. Bobby struggled as hard as he could and it took the strength of both vets plus two members of staff to hold him still. Susan was told to restrain him by laying across his neck and holding the head up - that way he would not be able to struggle so much. A bucket of clear water was brought and the young Australian vet began the job of putting to rights Bobby's teeth problems. As soon as the rasp touched his teeth, Bobby almost went berserk. It was all they could do to restrain him. Mr. Harry and Mr. David took turns at filing, then dipping the file into the water and so on. All the time they worked, Bobby was in a complete turmoil. He had panicked and there were none of his friends there to assist him. He thought the vets were going to kill him and the rasp made the whole of his head vibrate. It was a slow job but, as Mr. Harry explained, it had to be done for the pony's sake. Bobby vowed he would never like or trust another human again.

The files ground on and on and the pony started to sweat. He hated the taste of blood in his mouth and was quite convinced his tongue was being cut out! Every now and then the vets stopped to see how their work was progressing. Wads of unchewed grass were trapped in the cheeks of the old pony and these were cleared. It was obvious that this treatment had been carried out just in time. A few months more and it could have been too late.

After what to Bobby seemed for ever, Mr. David announced that he thought they had completed their work and Mr. Harry agreed. The ropes were taken off. The mistake they made however was to put Bobby back into the paddock where the others were grazing. Unlike Bluff who could take a bit of pain, Bobby was just the reverse. He wanted the whole world to know how they had treated him and as soon as he was released he galloped across to Bruce. Quickly he told his brother the grizzly tale. Poor Bruce. He could not believe what he was being told. Bobby gabbled everything out and emphasised how much it had hurt and how the vets had tried to kill him. He went into great detail of all the blood that was around and how Susan had tried to strangle him and all the nasty things he could think of. His story was so bad that when Susan came out to collect Bruce, the poor old grey ran for his life. In no way was he going to let them put him through so much pain. Susan could not understand this usual placid pony but as the vets were waiting, she summoned help and eventually Bruce was caught.

On the walk out of the paddock, he was absolutely paralysed with fear. His knees trembled so much that twice he stumbled. The sight that caught his eye was frightening. There were two figures dressed in long white coats with a few staff members standing around and the tools of their trade looked very awesome to the poor old pony as he approached. The ropes were put on after a struggle and Bruce was lowered to the ground. He found that Susan with her arms around his neck calmed him a little and as soon as the rasp started its work, the feeling was horrible but not as bad as Bobby had said. True, he could taste blood and the file on the teeth did vibrate through his skull. Although Bruce found it most uncomfortable, he did not experience actual pain. Now and again, when the file touched the wrong spot, he kicked a bit but that was out of nervous reaction and not spite. Bruce decided that it was not a pleasant experience but it was nowhere near the grotesque picture that Bobby had conjured up.

As soon as it was over, Susan made a great fuss of him as she led him back to the paddock. He had to admit his mouth did feel sore but not too bad. Bobby rushed up to him. "Did the butchers do their worst with you Bruce?" he snorted and Bruce had to tell him that through his brother's exaggeration, he had been frightened to death! Bobby was visibly shaken. At least he expected Bruce to vow his hatred of all humans, especially vets, but instead, here he was saying that they had only done their best. Bobby was quite sure they had done something to Bruce's brain.

It was not too long before their sore mouths were a thing of the past and the two greys could enjoy the grass again.

Chapter 18

Gala Day

As the summer wore on, the first happy day for Don was when he once again joined his three friends in the big paddock and together they trotted around as a group. Don soon forgot the many days of misery he had endured in the small paddock and when he was brought in to the stable at night, he made a point of not looking across at his prison.

The ponies sensed that something was up when they looked over the fence and saw a man with a tractor mowing the paddock next door and then rolling the turf.

Cocky explained that it was 'gala' time again and for the next few weeks, everything would be hustle and bustle whilst the staff prepared for the big day. The ponies asked what it was for and Cocky told them he did not know but would make enquiries and would tell them when he had found out. He discovered that Gala Day was when the staff entertained a lot of people in the Sanctuary from outside to raise cash to pay for all the food the animals ate and for all the other things necessary to run the centre and that cost a lot of money. Don pointed out that to feed him would not cost a lot of money because they never gave him very much to eat!

Bobby enquired why people needed the thing called "money" and as none of the ponies could tell him, they politely ignored the question. Cocky went on to explain that the chickens which were there last year, had to be locked up all day. People came to peer at them in their cages and they had ended up full of food with the numerous titbits that had been thrown to them. Don said he thought they should have more of these Gala Days and emphasised that he, for one, was looking forward to it.

The paddock adjoining the ponies' pasture was the centre point for carts, wagons, agricultural implements, bunting and all manner of items and equipment. Bruce remarked that it looked like a rubbish dump and not at all like the paddock in which they had previously grazed for so long.

During the next few days, members of staff raked up the grass and filled in holes to make the field ready. Each day, they had an audience of ponies all eager to learn just what was going on. Cocky Bantam kept them well informed on progress each night and he also told them of the names of things that were being set up which the ponies had never seen or heard of before. Tents and marquees sprang up and flags and bunting fluttered from every building which, to a pony, was a little frightening, especially when the wind blew, they made a noise. The whole centre was transformed from a nice quiet home-loving Sanctuary to a noisy, colourful place where nothing looked the same. The ponies felt a little scared as they were led from stable to paddock each day and all of them, except Don, hoped that it would soon be over. Don stood every night dreaming of people handing him food all day and Susan not being able to do a thing about it!

One evening when Cocky arrived, he said to Bluff:

"Th'day after tomorrow's the big day!"

"How do you mean?" enquired Bluff.

"It's the big day" repeated Cocky "you know, the Gala Day!"

"Oh, is it?" said Bluff.

"Yes it is" went on Cocky "and that is the day that yours

truly makes himself scarce!"

"Why is that?" asked Bluff sounding all pathetic.

"Because" said Cocky "all the flipping people come trooping in here and the noise is unbearable!"

"Where will you go?" queried Bruce, who had been standing listening intently.

"I don't know yet" said Cocky "but it will be miles away from people, especially the little ones!"

"Don't you like the little people?" asked Bobby.

"Not on your life" Cocky chirped. "Those little devils spend all their time chasing little animals and scaring them half to death! Susan won't be able to stop them either.." he added. "She will be in the Sanctuary seeing to the whims of all the old dears who come to spend their money!"

"Who will be looking after us then? questioned Bobby.

"You!" answered Cocky. "You will be looking after yourselves or else they will send some little person who they call a "voluntary". A voluntary knows nothing whatsoever of your wants and needs and how to look after you."

"That sounds awful" said Bluff not very happy about what he was hearing.

"It isn't" echoed Cocky. "On Gala Day, it's everyone for himself and if you take a tip from me, you want to keep as far away from your doors as you can."

"If we do that" interjected Don "we won't get any titbits to eat and that will spoil the day for me."

"Why do you suggest we stand away from our doors?" enquired Bluff sensibly.

"If you don't" warned Cocky " all you will get are thousands of smelly hands reaching out to clout you on the head!"

"Ugh" thought Bluff.

"You know, you have scared the living daylights out of us"

said Bruce.

"Oh, have I?" was the reply. "Sorry mates!" and with that the bantam flew up to sleep in his favourite spot in the rafters.

None of the ponies slept much that night. Don considered he would miss out on his titbits. Bluff and Bruce had been thoroughly scared by what Cocky had said and poor Bobby, as usual, was frightened by anything.

As soon as dawn was welcomed by the birds, sounds of activity started in the Sanctuary. Voices were coming from all sides and it took a little courage for the ponies to venture to their doors and look out. To their surprise they saw people everywhere with cars, vans and all manner of other vehicles. The ponies came in for extra attention later when they were taken one by one back from the paddock to the stables and given a bath. This did not suit Don who stamped and kicked and in general made a nuisance of himself. "I'm always the first for any of these acts of torture" he snorted and did his utmost to keep out of the way of the water. Susan worked up a good lather and made the small black pony annoyed. "You are getting your own back for the way I threw you out of my hell-hole" he spluttered between mouthfuls of shampoo. "I really hate you, you mean, vicious, wench!" he went on. But it was no use. Susan could not understand a word he was saying and to her he was just protesting at having a bath. Whilst he was being dried off, his mane was pulled and his tail was trimmed and at the end of it all, he looked superb! He raged about being made up to look more like a filly and in all the years he had worked underground, none of the miners had treated him like this "what would the others think of him looking and smelling this way!" Don was a picture of misery and when the time came to be put back into the paddock, the first thing he did was to have a good roll. "That will teach you and your rotten bath!" he fumed at the retreating Susan but she never minded him rolling because it would soon brush off.

The other ponies, whilst not enjoying the beauty treatment, took it in their stride and at the end of the session, they all looked like new lads, but not one of them mentioned anything about their appearance. Not, that is, until a fluttering at Bluff's door heralded Cocky Bantam.

"Whew" he cackled. "What's that horrible smell!" and looking over at Bluff, he nearly fell off the door with laughter. "What on earth have they done to you Ducky?" he said. "Oh, you do look nice!"

"That's enough!" replied Bluff, hoping that the bantam would not go on with the conversation. But his hope was dashed.

"I have never seen such pretty ponies" Cocky went on, after walking around the stall and having a look at the two greys who were huddled together, trying not to look conspicuous. "My, my" he went on. "Aren't we just the thing! All you lot need now are ribbons in your manes and WOW - anything could happen!"

The ponies were very embarrassed and would willingly have throttled the loud-mouthed bantam!

"I must nip next door and have a look at old fatty!" he said but Don took exception to this suggestion.

"You just stay where you are!" he shouted.

"Not on your life! Come on, me old Don, let's have a look at you" and with that the bird fluttered out of Bluff's stall and on to Don's door.

"Wowee" he exclaimed as he saw Don standing as far back in his stall as he could.

"You look absolutely T-E-R-R-I-F-I-C" Cocky expounded

"you are more pretty than your sisters next door!" and with that Don could not control himself any longer. He charged across the stall at the sarcastic bantam who was strutting up and down. The sight of Don moving like streak-lightning caused Cocky to leap up in the air and lose a few feathers!

How Don missed him the bantam would never know but he had to fly out of the stable area before regaining his composure.

"You spiteful twit" he called back. "You have no sense of humour have you" and he had to admit the old black pony had put the wind up him a bit.

"No, I haven't" called Don. "And if you come here again with your mickey taking attitude, I'll do it again!"

"Like heck you will" replied an angry Cocky who was adjusting his feathers before flying back on Bluff's door.

"I'm not going to give you that chance mate!" Bluff showed no sympathy for the bantam when he flew back on to his door.

"That friend of yours nearly killed me" complained Cocky in a very hurt voice.

"I can understand why" Bluff retorted. "You have been very rude to all of us since you arrived. We will not put up with too much of it" he went on, letting the bantam know that his type of humour was not always acceptable to the ponies.

"What!" the bantam yelled. "Me rude! You must be joking. There you are, all looking absolutely beautiful with a sheen on your coats that makes 'Cherry Blossom' look dull and you say I am rude? How on earth do you make that out?"

"Well you are!" replied Bluff. "You never seem to know if you are being rude or not!"

"Now look here my old silver!" Cocky murmured in his silky voice. "You know that I wouldn't hurt you, don't you.

Remember when you had your bad accident? Wasn't it I who flew straight here to see that you were all right? Isn't it me who brings you all the up to date info on what's happening in this place? Don't I sleep in your stall 'cos I like you most?"

"Oh, shut up Cocky!" Bluff interrupted. "Flattery will get you nowhere!"

"All right then Bluff" Cocky replied softly, with his head low "I don't suppose you will want to know what is going to happen in the morning, will you?"

"What's that?" asked Bluff showing interest again. "No, no. I will only be accused of flattery if I tell you!" retorted Cocky sarcastically.

"Oh come on" said Bluff. "Stop messing about or I will knock you off my door like my friend did next door."

"There you go again" whined Cocky. "Because I am only a little creature and because you're bigger than me, you always use force, or threaten to!"

"Don't bother with that little creep!" shouted Don, still vexed with the bantam.

"Excuse me Bluff" went on Cocky "I think your sister spoke!"

"I'll 'sister' you when I get you" roared Don and even the greys thought that Cocky had overdone his rudeness to Don.

Cocky somehow sensed that the ponies were mad at him so without preening any more, he flew up into the roof. It was sometime before any of them spoke and then it was Cocky who remarked that tomorrow really was the Gala Day and it was as if a dam had been breached! All the ponies spoke together "THE GALA?"

"Yes" replied a tired Cocky. "In the morning it all happens and then for the whole day you will be bombarded by people who will come and look at you as if you are freaks.." he went on. "Some even wave things in front of you to see if you are blind!"

"What's blind?" enquired Bluff. Cocky mentioned that he had heard one of the staff saying a lot of people thought that because the ponies had worked for so long underground, they would be blind. "You know, not able to see" explained the bantam.

"Do you mean" questioned Bruce "that people think that it is dark in the pits?"

"Well, it would seem so" answered Cocky.

"Don't they know that with electric lights, in some places it is as light as it is on the surface?" queried Bobby.

"All I know is" said Cocky "that tomorrow a lot of people will come along and test you all to see if you can see!"

"I shall pretend that I am blind" put in Don.

"And when they throw titbits in to you, you will not be able to see them will you?" asked Bluff.

"Well, maybe I will pretend that I can see only a little bit" Don replied.

"Just enough to see the food being thrown at you!" remarked Bruce.

"Yes, that's right" agreed Don. "Just enough to see that..." and all the ponies chuckled at the devious black pony.

That evening, instead of the Sanctuary being quiet, the place was alive with activity and noise. The ponies spent most of the time peering out of their stalls, trying to see all the coming and goings. There were cars bringing things in. A man came to erect some boxes on poles through which a voice could be heard shouting similar words to those they heard at the welcoming ceremony. "One, Two, Three, testing, testing...." and then music could be heard just as it did when the pitmen carried a little box in their hands whilst waiting to go on shift. Susan was not around and the only people the ponies recognised were Old Portly and a man they knew as Stan, who Cocky reported was the 'geezer' who was in charge of the Gala. The man Stan had a habit of putting a kind of box up to his face when he was looking at the ponies and then he would laugh and say "That was a good one" which left all the ponies very puzzled. Don called him 'Baldy' number two because he was almost as bald on top as Bill the gardener. Although he had strange ways, the ponies thought Stan was rather kind. Sleep was a long time coming because of all the hustle and bustle going on but none of the ponies would have slept much because of the excitement. A slow snoring up in the roof told them that the bantam was in a deep sleep and most probably dreaming of Don.

Before dawn had really broken, the ponies and Cocky were rudely awaked by Susan with a "Come on you lazy lot, wakey, wakey.." and a clashing of buckets which by any standards would not be welcome. A clucking up in the roof caused the girl to glance up and catch sight of Cocky. Before he could make his escape, a well-aimed broom handle dislodged the bantam right into her arms. "Le'go you snide!" yelled Cocky fluttering his wings as best he could. "Le'go you, you, you snooty woman!" It was no good. He was well and truly tucked under Susan's arm as she marched off towards the hen house with Cocky's voice still calling her all the wicked names he could think of and getting fainter and fainter in the distance.

Susan still had a smile on her face of someone who had just won a great victory when she returned to the stable block. "This time" she was saying to no one in particular "this time that little rascal is NOT going to get me into trouble with the Captain."

As soon as breakfast was over, the ponies were tied up outside their stalls and the other girls came and brushed and curry-combed them whilst Susan cleaned their stables. There was an air of great excitement around the place and in the morning sunshine, with all the flags and bunting in place, the Sanctuary looked a picture. Bill the gardener had cut all the lawns and the flowers around the stable block looked beautiful. As staff came and went, all the ponies heard them say was "Isn't it a lovely day for the Gala!" It seemed that it was most important for the weather to stay dry and fine.

As the ponies were being groomed, they were watching the arrival of more and more people laden with all sorts of things. Some had flowers, some old clothes, others had tins and bottles and others just hustled and bustled all over the place. The sun rose higher in the sky and out of the strange boxes set on the poles, came soft music which the ponies rather enjoyed. It helped reduce Don's anger at having his hooves painted black and some ribbons put in his mane. Bluff had to stifle a giggle because the ribbons Don was wearing were red and they stood out very prominently on his black mane. Bluff, a Cream Dun, with his creamy beige coat and dark brown mane and tail, had yellow ribbons. They did not seem to be so bright against his colouring. The greys both had blue ribbons, which with their colouring, contrasted very well. None of the ponies mentioned the ribbons because to them it was a bit degrading. But the humans wanted their fun, so who were they to object! Bluff was also glad that Cocky was not around. Had the bantam said anything to Don, Bluff feared the little black pony would have run amok.

All the staff looked smart and the Captain surprised them all by arriving in his army uniform. At first they did not recognise him but as soon as he spoke, they knew who it was.

"They look absolutely spiffing" he said, pointing to the ponies. "Well done there, well done..." and with military precision, he marched off.

"What was that all about?" asked Bruce, his eyes following the retreating Captain.

"Search me" replied Bluff "he must have been pleased about something."

"The man's an idiot" cried Don, trying desperately to peer over the top of his stall.

"Why do you say that?" queried Bluff, still keeping an eye on the retreating Captain.

"Well" said Don "he comes breezing in, looking all important, makes one statement which makes no sense to any of us, then breezes off again." Bluff thought Don was being a little hard on the poor man who, after all, was instrumental in arranging this lovely home for them.

"The Captain is a nice man really" Bluff went on "he has put a lot of work into making us feel at home here."

"Rubbish" snapped Don. "He is never here. All he does is issue orders like 'do this' or 'do that' to the others and they run around in little circles, especially that Portly twit."

Bluff could not be bothered with Don's outbursts. He had always been the same. Nothing ever pleased him or was ever right, no matter how hard the people tried. Bruce told him off for being rude and the matter was dropped. It was not a day for arguments but they all knew that unless Don's stomach was 'seen to', then everything would be wrong.

The amount of people in the Sanctuary grew by the minute and all of them came to the stables to see the 'famous four.' Music was still being played on the pole 'things'. Stan caused the ponies to laugh when he appeared with the Captain for he was wearing a funny red hat with a tassle on it.

"What a berk" commented Don.

"I think it does something for him" said Bobby.

"So do I" laughed Don, trying hard not to snort too much. Susan came to the stables and immediately Don remarked that she had actually combed her hair and looked particularly smart. The other ponies had to agree with him this time because Susan really did look different and she smelt as though she had tipped perfume all over herself.

"That smell she has is nice" commented Bluff. "Yes, as long as she doesn't get too close to you" Don replied "although I prefer her normal smell..."

"Don't be so rude!" Bluff told him.

Susan had changed into her best uniform because she would have to help on one of the stalls later on and although she never knew what the ponies were saying about her, she guessed it was something rude!

All the little animals that usually wandered about during the day had been locked up for their own safety and the ponies could hear the noise they made drifting across from their pens. The first of the titbits arrived and Don was at the door, his mouth dribbling with expectation. Just as a lady was going to offer him a treat, a man standing beside her said: "Look, Ethel, it says 'not to feed the ponies.' "

"Oh, go on Albert" cried the lady "they won't know about this little once."

"Oh yes they will " replied Albert with a hint of authority in his voice.

"Why don't you shut your mouth" snorted Don, making an attempt to nip the silly man's fingers as he tried to pat him on the head.

Looking over the door in Bruce and Bobby's stall was a very fat lady who had no teeth and the mere sight of her frightened the life out of the two greys. "Hey Bluff" called Bruce "we've got a right funny looking old dear outside our place. She must be the ugliest thing we've ever seen!"

"Well you keep her there then" replied Bluff and he heard the lady saying "Come on my loves, come and have a kiss" and Bluff smiled knowing that the invitation itself would make them both feel sick!

"What are you doing about her" called out Don, having cooled down a bit since Albert's departure.

"Oh we are not looking at her" replied Bobby. "We have got our backs to her."

"Make sure she doesn't climb over the door" smirked Don, trying to frighten them more.

"Don't say things like that" said Bruce and then to Bobby "Turn round and have a look."

"Not on your sweet life" answered Bobby, moving closer to Bruce.

The fat old lady moved along to Bluff and reading his name on his door called "Come on then Bluffy, Wuffy. Come to your Mum!"

"My what?" cried Bluff and he could hear the others laughing their heads off.

"Come and have a kiss" the voice went on. "Come and let Mummy see what a nice boy you are" to which Bluff had to laugh and say: "Not on your sweet life madam! Not on your sweet life!"

It was Don's turn next and he went forward a few paces just to see if she had anything to eat but when he found she had nothing, he turned his back towards her and passed wind. "You filthy little creature" she shouted and stormed off leaving behind four ponies almost crying with laughter and telling Don what a rotten trick it was to play on her.

There were scores of people milling around the stables and the noise grew louder and louder. The throngs of people wanted to see what pit ponies looked like and the ponies all felt a little out of place being stared at so intently. Most of the time, they took Cocky's advice and stood well away from the door as the slapping on the head and neck hurt quite a bit; had they bitten anybody, they would have been in trouble.

After a while, the people were cleared from the stable doors and Susan with some more girls in uniform came in with brand new halters and lead ropes, all made in the same colours as the ribbons they were wearing. The halters were securely fitted to each pony and tested before the ponies walked out. At first, the bright sunshine hurt their eyes and their limbs were a little stiff after being in the stables for so long. As they walked, however, they acclimatised and found the warm sun on their backs really pleasant. The crowds of people were more than the ponies had ever seen and they seemed to be everywhere. With a girl in front clearing a way, they were walked out into their paddock which none of them recognised and into an area all roped off which seemed the only place where people were not allowed. Everyone clapping their hands made an awful din! Don was behaving very well, mainly because he was overcome by the numbers of humans.

"Ladies and Gentlemen" said the voice coming from the top of the pole: "We are proud to present to you four pit ponies who have come to us in the last year and who are now installed in the Sanctuary as residents."

Don had never seen a pole with a strange contraption on top of it speak before and was quite amazed. The crowds banged their hands together and shouted. It was all too much for the fearsome four. After the voice had gone they were walked around the edge of the crowds of people and all they could see was a mass of clawing hands all wanting to touch them. The ponies were on their best behaviour, however. As they went round they met for the very first time a horse, not a small horse but a big Shire horse.

" 'ello little'un" he said to Don. "This yer first year 'ere?"

"Err, err, yes-s" stammered a bewildered Don "I-it i-s"

"Wot 're yer doin'then, giving rides?" the Shire asked.

"N-no, w-well a-at least I don't think s-so." replied Don, who was absolutely amazed at the size of the Shire.

"Wot yer mean yer on'y fink so?" enquired the big fellow with a distinct cockney accent which Don could not understand.

"No I didn't say I think so" said Don "I said I didn't think so" and he was glad that just at the moment, the Shire was moved on.

"Did you lot see that?" cried the little black pony "it was a horse!"

"You surprise me" returned Bluff "I thought it was a mountain!"

They all had a good giggle. Further on, they saw some more Shire horses and some donkeys. (Bruce asked one what it was - which was how they knew they were "donkeys.") Bobby thought they looked like ponies 'gone wrong' but no other explanation was given.

Don looked around, hoping that he would not have to meet the old cockney Shire horse again but his luck was not in because a voice behind him called:

"Hey, shorty" and a cold shiver ran down Don's spine. He looked round and there coming up on him fast was the enormous Shire horse.

"D-did y-you c-call?" he asked in a trembling voice.

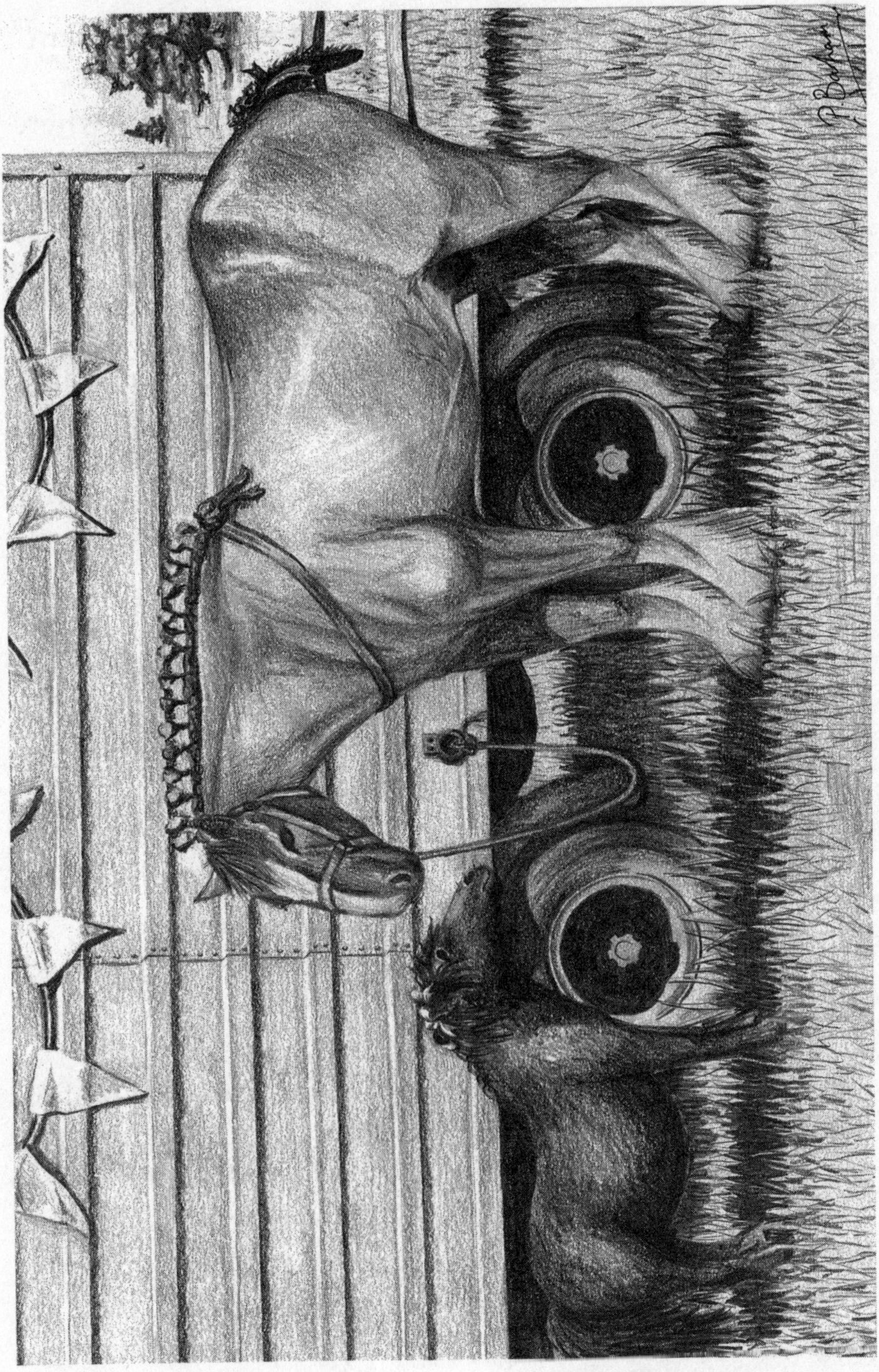

"Yus mate" replied the Shire "Where d'yer 'ang aht then?"

"Ang aht?" questioned Don. "What's 'ang aht' then?"

"'Dahn't be s'daft" replied the horse. "Yer nah - where d'live?"

"Oh, where do I live?" mimicked Don. "Oh, I live here."

"Live 'ere??" questioned his protagonist "whereabarts 'ere?"

"In the stables here" returned Don trying to kill the conversation.

"Wot abart them uvers then?" queried the Shire, nodding at the other three.

"They live here as well" volunteered Don.

"Y've go' it made mate, ain't yer?" said the Shire with a hint of jealousy in his voice. "Thar's me 'n me mates 'aving t' give these rotten kids rides all day whilst yer lot lord it up on us."

"No we don't do that" replied a scared Don.

"'How d'yer know?" asked the Shire.

"I don't" returned Don and was thrilled to be led away from the inquisitive old Shire.

"I think he liked you Don" commented Bruce, pleased that it was Don the Shire had taken a fancy to.

"Well, I can't say I liked him a lot" said Don feeling quite pleased with the way he had handled the situation.

"We noticed that you were most polite to the dear old horse!" teased Bluff.

"I blooming well had to be!" returned Don.

A while later they were led back to the stables and after their scares out in the paddocks, it was the first time that they were glad to be inside rather than out. People still thronged around their stable doors and even Don kept at the back of the stall to dodge the avalanche of outstretched hands, all wanting to slap them on the head. Food was scarce as all the nice people read the signs and never attempted to feed the ponies.

Don discovered a nastier type of human who would offer him anything but as the thing he took was hot and burnt his mouth, he joined the others in keeping well out of the way.

It was late when the noise started to abate and the people thinned out. The ponies were all hungry and looked forward to their tea but whilst the crowds outside remained, there would be little chance of that and it gave Don a reason for moaning about what a rotten day it had been.

As soon as the people had left, Susan came round with the tea and a welcome sight she was too. There was very little conversation about the day's events and it only livened up when the fluttering of wings announced Cocky Bantam's arrival on Bluff's door.

"Wotcha matey!" he cackled "had a good day have yer?"

The question was greeted with a stony silence.

"Oh dear" he went on "we didn't have a good day then?" Still he drew no response from the stalwart four.

"Who upset you then?" he tried again.

"YOU" was the unanimous reply.

"Why me?" queried Cocky.

"Because you've come back, you, you..." said Don.

"Oh dear. That big Shire horse didn't do you much good did it?" retorted Cocky.

"How do you know about that?" asked Don, a little surprised at the bantam's knowledge of what had gone on.

"Never mind how I know!" exclaimed Cocky. "The point is I do know and I heard that you were more than polite to him!"

"No I wasn't" replied Don, not wanting this tiresome bird to get the better of him.

"I'm sorry to say" Cocky continued "it's all around the Sanctuary that you nearly wet yourself when he came up!"

"Don't be so disgusting" spat Don, trying to stop the conversation before it became embarrassing. But Cocky was not going to let him off the hook that easily!

"That great horse put the wind up you Don. All the hens in the hen-house know it to be true."

"Actually," said Don now trying to retrieve the situation "we got on very well. He asked me a few questions and I in turn asked him a few" he went on, trying to sound important.

"You mean he asked you and you blubbered some kind of reply!" answered Cocky.

"Whenever you two meet there is always trouble" interposed Bluff, trying to calm the situation.

"Yes and this feathery little twit always starts it!" put in Don, feeling a little hurt because he had lost this particular argument with Cocky.

"Now then" said Bluff "don't start up again." Bruce tried to break up the quarrel by asking the others what they thought of the Gala Day and instantly Bluff stated that it was wonderful for the people but for the animals it was terrible and he hoped they did not have too many of such events in a year.

"They only have one" said Cocky, breaking off his nightly preen to join in the conversation.

"Well, that's a relief" replied Bruce. "I don't think I could stand more than that!"

"Nor could Old Portly" went on Don, feeling that he should at least contribute something on this new topic of conversation. "Did you see the poor old devil. He was walking around like a zombie." Bluff considered that it was not nice to call Old Portly names. After all, he was the Manager of the place and they should really have some respect for him.

"Oh, we do" laughed Don "we think he's stupid!" and he

was joined by the greys and Cocky in his sniggering.

"I think that you are all unkind" Bluff reminded them. "You call the Captain names, the gardener names, Stan the Gala man gets criticised and now you ridicule the Manager. I think it's disgraceful!"

"Ere, ere" put in Cocky. "We will not be disrespectful to any of the idiots again" and the stables erupted with snorts and giggles of laughter. Even Bluff had to smile and he realised that they did not really mean all the nasty things they said - well, not quite all of them.

Chapter 19

Full Circle

The ponies settled down very well after the Gala although it was some weeks before they were able to wander into the paddock that had been used for all the events. It seemed there were many things dropped there that could be harmful such as the plastic and metal rings off cans, broken bottles and plastic bags, as well as polystyrene drinking cups.

Eventually the ponies were given both paddocks to roam in and their lives returned to normal. The long sunny days of summer continued into autumn, when once again the nights grew longer and early frosts appeared.

One evening when they had settled in their stalls Cocky flew in and said something that surprised them.

"Do you realise that in two weeks time you will have been in the Sanctuary for one whole year?" Cocky remarked.

The stables went silent. Not one of the ponies had thought anything about their length of time there and to be told it was one year was unbelievable.

Bluff spoke first. "Do you know fellows" he said "it doesn't seem possible that we have been in our new home all this time."

"It seems like eternity to me" complained Don. "I feel that I have been a prisoner here all my life."

"Oh do shut up" said Bruce. "Try to be serious for a moment!"

"I am" complained Don.

"No you are not" returned Bruce. "You are expressing a personal grievance that has nothing to do with how long we have been here." He went on "it has been a marvellous year and I have enjoyed every minute of it. I hope that I may be able to spend many more years here..."

"So say I" agreed Bluff. "It has been good. We have had some laughs and we have had some tears but on the whole, it has been terrific!"

Don could not see why they were getting sentimental about the year that had just gone by. To him, it had been a year of "don't do this .." or "don't do that. You can't eat this or you can't eat that. You can't go in this paddock or you can't have hay-nets." It was all misery. The only bright thing about it was his battles with Susan and Cocky - but they were not that exciting really.

Bobby had been doubtful in the beginning but as time went on, he realised what a good home they had come to and was very glad he could continue sharing a stable with Bruce.

Bluff asked Cocky what he thought of their first year in the Sanctuary and of course the bantam answered immediately saying that apart from their pinching his best roosting spot, he thought they had been good company, except for old fatty who, in Cocky's estimation, "..was a born pessimist!"

Bluff thought they should reminisce on the year and asked them all to think of the loyal service that Susan had given them despite traumatic incidents with Don, who should not be forgiven for the way he had treated her. Bluff felt that Cocky could have been more pleasant to her as well.

"Oh, it's all right for you to talk" said Cocky "you have never had two feet of broom handle pushed up your backside -especially when the perch you were on was, to say the least, very precarious!"

"That's no excuse for the names you called her" put in Bruce.

"Coming from you" answered Cocky "whom I have heard call a few people names, that is rather like the kettle calling the pot black."

"What's he talking about?" asked Bobby.

"He is talking about kettles and pots" returned Bruce "which has no relevance to our conversation at all."

"'course it does" snapped Cocky. "It's a saying the humans use."

"Well, I've never heard of it" replied Bruce.

"Nor I" mumbled Bobby, who was getting quite perplexed by the conversation.

Bluff stood quietly in his stall, his mind slowly going through the events of the year. The ups and downs that life had brought them; after all, it was a gigantic move they had all made after spending so many years doing a set job every day. Then to find themselves in a changed situation to which they had to acclimatize was not easy for the four. The friends they had made had been marvellous. Bluff thought of Cocky Bantam who, for all his ways, was indeed a very loyal friend and his mind raced back to the time they had chased the fox just to help the bantam. The cows, for all their faults, had brought to the ponies another dimension in their lives which they had had to cope with and they had succeeded too, despite the attack on Bluff. Bluff smiled to himself when he thought of the time when Don and Cocky had caused so much confusion at the welcoming ceremony and he pictured the Captain hopping around, holding his fingers and using the most terrible language. Seeing Bruce almost given up for dead under the roof of the stables was a memory that Bluff was not too keen to remember, along with the vision of himself being brought back from the dead at the water trough. It had been an eventful year at South Bunford.

While Bluff stood, head bowed, going over their life at the centre, Don was getting very agitated trying to keep his thoughts to himself.

"How" he mused "can that windblown Bluff say anything nice about that jumped up slip of a girl who is supposed to look after us. She has treated me like nothing on this earth ..." and as he went on thinking, he became more and more agitated until, without realising it, he found himself actually kicking the side of the stall!

"Hey up in there!" called Bluff, being brought back to reality with a bump. "What on earth are you up to?"

Don felt stupid. He could not tell them what he had been thinking.

"I slipped" he mumbled, trying hard to sound convincing.

"What, on your stomach?" quipped Bruce to which the others smirked out loud.

"Don't be so rude" snapped Don, feeling worse now because he thought he had said the wrong thing.

Cocky Bantam woke up at the commotion and started to preen himself dropping, in the process, an unwanted feather on to Bluff who was standing below.

"You lot make me laugh" he said. "Here you all are, been in this place a year and still fighting like cat and dog."

Another feather swayed down from above. Bluff felt like saying something but thought better of it. He did not want to give Cocky a reason for babbling through the night.

Both the greys were restless; they had kept out of the arguments that evening although each had in mind pictures of events they had witnessed over the last year. To both of them Freedom and Light had been the greatest present they could have been given and both were grateful for it. All the things that had happened to them at the centre over the previous year were placed in two parts within their minds. The good and the bad. It was strange but on this night it was the good things, the mischievous things that were uppermost in their thoughts.

Bluff, Bruce and Bobby knew that Don and Cocky Bantam would always argue, but that was a part of their new way of life. Without Cocky, the nights and days to come would be very boring. To the ponies, it was a new chapter in their lives, a chapter that would go on day in and day out here at South Bunford.

As the dusk gave way to the night and silence descended in the stable block, there was an atmosphere which told anyone who was passing, that despite all the friendly bickering and insults, there had come to that remote part of Surrey a new and exciting partnership, not only between the bantam and the ponies but also between all the other animals that made up the complex. The ponies knew that after their long and arduous toil in the mines they had found what was for them a new home. A home where the 6.00 am siren was missing; a home where the clanging of the pithead shaft was gone for ever and in this home they had freedom. Freedom to roam in the paddocks, mix with the other animals and enjoy a retirement that no one would, or could, say they did not justly deserve.